Still Life
with Books

Simon Lane

Still Life
with Books

a novel

Simon Lane

Bridge Works Publishing Co.
Bridgehampton, New York

Library of Congress Cataloging-in-Publication Data

Lane, Simon, 1957–
    Still life with books : a novel / Simon Lane.—1st ed.
      p. cm.
    ISBN 1-882593-02-2 (hard cover : acid-free paper)
    I. Title.
  PR6062.A5324S75   1993
  823'.914—dc20   93–18948
                                         CIP

10 9 8 7 6 5 4 3 2 1

The jacket art is a reproduction of Vincent van Gogh's painting *Still Life with Books* (*stilleven met boeken*), 1888. Grateful acknowledgment is made to the Vincent van Gogh Foundation/Van Gogh Museum, Amsterdam, for permission to publish this reproduction.

Book and jacket design by Edith Allard

Printed in the United States of America

First Edition

To Slim

To lose one parent, Mr. Worthing, may be regarded as a misfortune; to lose both looks like carelessness.
—*Wilde*

Memory is an act of the imagination.
— *Borges*

contents

prologue

The cover of this book is a detail of a painting
by Vincent van Gogh, the greatest painter
who ever lived. My friend, Harm, selected it
for me. In fact, the last thing he did before being sent up was to hand me a postcard from
the Van Gogh Museum, Amsterdam, illustrat-
ing the painting and, on its reverse, giving
details:

Vincent van Gogh (1853–1890)
stilleven met boeken
parijs 1888—53 × 72.5 cm.

The reason van Gogh was the greatest
painter who ever lived is quite simple: he was
the most passionate. Harm told me that, for
van Gogh, subject matter was often an irrele-
vancy, that contrary to most twentieth-century
art, in which subject matter is *everything*, van
Gogh sought principally to inject his personality into the world around him. His genius

manifested itself in bringing matter to life, but the matter itself, in many ways, didn't matter.

This is an exaggeration, of course, like everything else. But Harm had a point. If we subordinate intention for a moment and stare, head on, at the facts, at material reality, we discover that all van Gogh needed to do to find a subject was to open his eyes. Whatever confronted him would suffice: a flower, a bottle, a tree, some roots, a chair, a field. Some books.

One of van Gogh's last paintings is a study of tree roots. It is a close-up of nature, a wild and violent painting that makes one think of the artist knee-deep in mud, squinting, seeking out more and more detail until his face is so close to nature that his nose actually touches it, in the same way in which his nose touches the canvas as he carves and hacks away at it with his palette knife. Yes, Harm was right: whatever else can be said, there is no doubt that van Gogh was passionate.

My decision to choose *stilleven met boeken* for this book's cover (based, it is fair to say, on Harm's initiative) should be seen in the light of the artist's decision to choose books for his subject matter. While the cover of van Gogh's painting might be said to consist of books, the cover of my book consists of a painting. I do not wish to give the impression that my decision is anywhere near as important as van Gogh's; it is obviously not, for van

Gogh was the greatest artist who ever lived (just look at his prices) while I am an author of fairly modest pretensions. My *boeken* will sell for $17.95, while van Gogh's *boeken* are worth a million times more. This is hardly inconsequential (as Harm, or any other art thief, might tell you), for in choosing *stilleven met boeken* as the cover of my novel, I am hoping that the value of my work will increase a little.

Van Gogh's books are wonderful things. Although open, we see no words. They are like the book I am starting now, just a pile of virgin paper stacked on the table. And yet the table on which the books are piled is the most exquisitely beautiful table ever made; it is covered with pink and white and cream paint and the shadows cast upon it by the books are green and blue and every shade in between.

In order to tell you all this, in order to describe van Gogh's painting, I am squinting, pressing my nose against the plastic-coated postcard so that my own shadow envelops it. I can almost make out a face reflected within its oily contours; I am now part of an open, empty book. I am lost, for as long as I like, within the hidden, simple mysteries of the greatest, most passionate painter who ever lived.

Still Life
with Books

brasserie dronenberg

Aldous Radice was actually killed by beer. We cannot, necessarily, lay the blame at the brewery door, so to speak; we cannot suggest, for example, that they immediately introduce wasp-proof bottles. That would be churlish. At the same time, we are at liberty to suggest that the Brasserie Dronenberg ("plus légère que jamais, plus forte encore pour le gars moderne") consider the advantages of placing a modest warning below its proud claims to have won every available beer trophy since the year of its founding, 1888: something to the effect that "modern guys" are not the only things attracted to its product, especially in summer, when any number of vile insects hover over the terrace table.

Death is always accompanied by irony of the "if only" school. Aldo's demise was no exception, for had I not already warned him, that blistering, Provençal afternoon, of the inherent dangers of drinking beer outside? "Thank you, Leonard! You saved my life!"

he exclaimed, as I put an arm out to stop him from drinking from his glass, having spied a wasp on its sticky inner rim.

I felt an upsurge of emotion at his words. What a good friend I was! Did not my action perfectly balance everything between us, so that the last vestiges of guilt I might have felt regarding Azadina were finally gone, evaporated into the thin air around us? What meaning, what profundity, what poignancy lay in saving the life of such an intimate, if elusive companion!

Alas, it is not only rare to be given the opportunity of saving someone's life, it is also rare to be made a party to that person's demise! How I curse the day now, how gravely do I regret the ornithological diversion I instigated, for was it not I who, pointing toward two swallows flirting over an adjacent birdbath, distracted Aldo's attention from his beer for a sufficient length of time, so that, upon reintroducing the glass to his thirsty lips, he failed to give it the very wasp check I had urged him to make five minutes earlier?

We must now make a slight alteration to our cover. The postcard, *stilleven met boeken*, now becomes part of a wider still life encompassing Aldous, now dead, his head slumped upon the pink and white and cream table, the shadow of his upturned nose cast, desultorily, over the ensemble. *Stilleven met boeken* should now read *stilleven met boeken met aldous.*

australia

It is 1991, a satisfying configuration, a numerical palindrome, the very stuff of logo-makers everywhere. Symmetrical beings, we like a little order. The world is something of a nuisance; neither round nor square, it surprises all but Columbus. Mercator and those other, diligent cartographers, have supplied us with fictional leaves for our diaries, so that planning trips abroad becomes apparently easier: thus, Greenland, which is not green, is larger than South America, which is not south at all, if one happens to be writing a book in Australia. Anyone who has offered a football as a gift and only partially succeeded in wrapping it for the nasty infant is perhaps acquainted with the problem.

Recently I have been feeling rather transparent. I think it has to do with the fact that people know too much about me. We are all a product of how others see us, and everyone at the moment appears to be looking at me accusingly and making judgments. I feel that this tells me more about their insecurities than about mine, but I have to admit that their constant, side-long glances unnerve me all the same. These people are driving me to distraction; they dress their prejudices with advice, and underneath their skin they have the desire to change me into some-one I do not wish to be.

For my part, I do not wish to change anything, simply arrest the motion, the continual, molecular bombardment, so that I will have enough time to be alone, with myself and my fantasies and, of course, with van Gogh, in the world he has created for me. My book will join the others on the pink and white and cream table, it will become part of the *stilleven met boeken met aldous*, and when that happens, it will be seen to have merged with its own cover.

My recent transparency has to do with the fact that I have been searching for truth in my life and have spent too much time trying to explain myself to people, when I should have been writing about Aldous and Azadina. I suppose I delayed this task because I felt so badly about Aldous, about his death. But, I ask you, how many times is one sup-posed to warn one's relative about wasps on any given summer's afternoon in Provence?

Sleeping with Azadina didn't help matters, ei-ther. What's the use of my trying to explain to people that it wasn't really I who made love to her that auspicious night ten years ago, but my licentious alter ego, whose constant erection always causes me such embarrassment at candle-lit dinner parties? How many times have I excused myself, walking backward into walls as I try desperately to avoid any number of outlandish shadows accompanying my ungainly exit?

This need to explain myself to others seems ridiculous in hindsight, now that I am on the other side of the world, looking up. When I was younger, I never had to do this, I made no effort, I felt no guilt, in fact I had not a care in the world. I was free. Now that I am 34, insecurity and doubt seem to characterize my existence to such an extent that I no longer feel I have any secrets, and my emotions swing back and forth like a metronome set on "sad." As a result, I feel the need to regress, to cover my tracks a little. Maybe that's why I came to Australia, because it's the last place on earth I thought I'd ever go. I can see things much more clearly now; I feel I am in a position to set it all down on paper. The solitude helps. Nobody knows I'm here. Not even the aboriginals.

Here I am, thinking about my place and my function in a world that seems to be revolving more around me than I around it. And the more I think, the more I realize that Aldous and Azadina have become an obsession and the only way I will be able to rid myself of it is by using the only means at my disposal: my ability to write. I must not be downcast. "Some grief shows much of love; but much of grief shows still some want of wit."

I am sitting at a desk in a strange apartment; I know that I will meet many people here as I fantasize, strange, ephemeral creatures whose presence I will be obliged to treat literally in order to keep my sanity. I see myself as a banished soul undergoing a kind of detoxification; I must be strong at all times.

A glass of mineral water sits at my side, its upturned meniscus reminding me of a childhood experiment in a physics lab. I have my box of HB pencils and my ream of paper; I bought them on the boulevard Saint-Michel on my way to the airport, thinking it would be my last chance to obtain writing materials. Who did I think I was? Van Gogh?

I reach up to turn on the standard lamp, and then I remember I could only have done that in my apartment in Paris. I have to pinch myself; I am in Australia and there is no standard lamp, just a big, open window with 24 hours worth of sky between me and what was France when I left it.

I know why I want to turn on the lamp: so that my shadow might come closer to me. The light is strong, the shadow well defined; it is actually streaming through the window, like a blessing. Suddenly, inexplicably, I am at peace with myself. I cannot now imagine what drove me to such depths of insecurity. I look at the person who was me, yesterday, and I look at someone else, who was me the day before. I strain my eyes, yet I fail to recognize all those different "me's" stretching into the past. But let us forget the past and concentrate on the "in-betweenness." And Aldo(us).

aldo(us)

It is 1991, some months earlier. We find ourselves in Paris, rather than Australia, accompanying Aldous Radice up the rue Bonaparte. His diary, removed from an inner pocket, testifies to an unusual, if uneventful life. Turning to April, we register a paucity of shaving soap. May is characterized by a canceled dinner with a question mark, while June and July, aside from several meteorological observations, including Hurricane Bob (who could equally have been a traveling companion), boast a number of theatrical outings. August, meanwhile, has a line running through its humid pages, annotated with the word "PARIS." Graphologists beware, for this is not the hand of Aldous but of his travel agent, who has done as she was bid, filling in the details, in a maternal fashion, with the aid of a red ballpoint and a ruler.

A gift from his Uncle Guillermo, who had received it, with compliments, from his bookmaker (Kagan and Kagan, Inc.), this diary now reveals the exact time of Aldous's appointment. Aldous looks at his watch once again before hurrying off.

As he does so, none of the people he passes could have imagined that the man in their midst had been diagnosed as having a "white speck" about one millimeter in diameter, situated ten centimeters to the rear of the left eye socket. But if they had, we could have reassured them, explaining that, despite the fact that further X-rays would have to be taken, there was no immediate cause for alarm. The question, as far as Aldous was concerned, was, like all questions, very simple. Was the white speck actually a particle of dust trapped during the radiographic process? Or was this "particle of dust" *inside* the cranium?

Assurances that there is no cause for alarm do nothing but cause alarm, and the alarm bells that provide the soundtrack for Aldous Radice's frenzied steps along the rue Bonaparte this afternoon ring outside as well as inside his head.

The only thing that never changes is the rule that states that no one ever changes. It is the exception to the rule that there are always exceptions. In the same way in which history can be said to repeat mistakes, people tend to reproduce their flaws throughout their lives, as if, somehow, they were playing to an audience, one that never ceased complaining, after each performance, that it hadn't quite gotten its money's worth.

Aldo, or Aldous, was a case in point. A rather tragic figure, deluded, lonely, dreaming to pass the time, he had always found his two names competed, so that he never quite knew what to call himself, let alone how to introduce himself to strangers. It seemed perfectly symbolic of the condition that had imposed itself upon him at the age of 11: orphanhood.

His parents had actually been killed by a demented band of Amazonian Indians, who had apparently mistaken them for another, more mythological couple, said to have been responsible, 12 centuries earlier, for the banishment of their ancestors from the banks of one tributary of the Amazon to the inner depths of a particularly desolate section of tropical rain forest. At least that's what came out at the inquest.

Aldous's mother was American; it is possible that she attended the series of Santa Barbara lectures given by Aldous Huxley in the late 1950s, although we cannot be sure. What we do know is that she was acquainted with the work of that lofty, myopic genius, whose experiments with pacifism and hallucinatory substances so shocked his contemporaries. Looking back in the direction of childhood, I do recall glimpsing a row of *H*s, for Huxley in the drawing room of the Radices' Ipanema apartment, when I visited my relatives in December 1968. It is therefore not surprising that the name of this English author should have been selected by my aunt, instead of a thousand others, possibly to encourage a literary and iconoclastic quality in her offspring. Either that, or it just seemed like a nice name.

His father was not of the same bent. A native of Milan, Salvatore Radice was a geologist and an entrepreneur of brilliance, who had established three alluvial gold mines in the Amazon basin and, as a result, amassed a small fortune by the late 1960s. It was while searching for a fourth that he and his wife (who, ironically, had pleaded with him to take her along) met their demise.

Salvatore's elder brother, Guillermo, my father, had also quit Europe upon graduating from university. Less gifted, more raffish, he had spent most of his student days at the San Siro racetrack and was, in fact, an accomplished, all-around gambler. I say this without prejudice, more in gratitude, for his abilities in that particular arena partially financed my college years. My father's move to New York City in September 1953 was certainly providential, and although I sometimes regret not having been brought up in Italy, I am moderately proud to call myself a New Yorker.

My uncle was not particularly impressed with the name "Aldous" when it was first mooted; indeed, a derisory puff of air was his reaction, repeated when the little creature popped out of its mother's womb in the spring of 1960.

"Al-dooss?" he exclaimed, upon being handed his mewling, puking son. "No, I shall call him Aldo, after Guillermo's friend, the Neopolitan gambler.

Half deafened by those damned alarm bells, which he still heard, and thought he would always hear, despite the fact that they had stopped ringing inside his head five minutes, five years, earlier, Aldous crossed the boulevard Saint-Germain and headed in a southerly direction, down the rue de Rennes, to meet his radiographic destiny. He put his fingers to his ears; was that the sound of waves crashing? Or was it the bell of a fire engine?

His accident had happened a week earlier, the very first day of his arrival in Gaul. Like all accidents, its sheer avoidability rendered it absurd. Since his parents' death, Aldous believed he had been living on borrowed time, which he would only return, like most debtors, when he was asked for it. He was, in short, a fatalist, which meant that accidents, such as the one that had occurred the preceding Wednesday (shampoo in the eye, soap under the heel) had already been planned years in advance, most probably when the bathroom of the friend of a friend's apartment had been installed. The only thing that worried him was the "particle of dust"; it did not accord with his ideas concerning destiny, for it was too arbitrary. To Aldous, fate was never arbitrary or accidental; it assumed a perfect, inescapable logic, without which all plans, however insignificant, would fall apart. Whether good or bad, joyous or melancholy, it had an obvious sense of purpose. Confusing signals were not its hall-marks.

So, what was going on? Exactly?

the brain

The brain is not subject to the same laws as other organs; it is undoubtedly rather anarchic. The principal difference is that it does not register pain, at least not in the same way as our lesser muscles. For this reason, astonishing results were obtained, mostly in North American hospitals, using only a local anesthetic, which is not, as Aldous thought up to the age of 13, an anesthetic administered "not far from home."

These appealing experiments took the form of operations on the brains of epileptics, who were invited to remain conscious during surgery. After introducing an opening to the cranium, certain key areas of the brain were stimulated with a spatula. In this way, depending on which sphere of the conscious or the subconscious had been brought to life, surgeons noted that the patient would be suddenly transformed, displaying behavior, emotional and often verbal, that clearly departed from conventional notions of time and place.

In the case of memory, which we know is capable of playing tricks, but which is not quite so accustomed to having tricks played upon *it*, the results were fascinating: the conscious patient, quite simply, removed him or herself from the strictures of the present and became more and more absorbed in past events, to such an extent that all the relevant emotions and sensations contingent to that reminiscence would come into play, repeated as accurately as if a scene from a film were being reenacted before their very eyes. The surgeons were, as you might imagine, quite dumbfounded at the sight of their patients laughing, crying, or otherwise exhibiting behavior not normally witnessed within the confines of their sterilized operating rooms.

Although this is no laughing matter, we are nevertheless, in the privacy of our own homes, permitted a chuckle as the docile patient, recalling a distant, amorous liaison, suddenly turns his head to the doctor at his side and whispers: "If you are coming, I will come with you, dearest."

But all this doesn't get us anywhere nearer Aldous and the waiting room.

Waiting rooms are all the same, empty spaces, magazines advertising sanitary napkins, children clicking their heels, dust falling.

"Esta sempre cheio de pò! Sempre! Sempre!" said Aldous mimicking Rosalia, the Radices' maid in Rio. "Yes, Rosalia. The dust does get everywhere. Even inside my head."

The young mother opposite looked down at her magazine and turned a crumpled page, nervously. "I don't like it when people talk to themselves," she said, to herself.

It was true to say that, since slipping on the soap, Aldous felt he had changed. It was hard to pinpoint, for it obviously coincided with his return to Paris after ten years' absence. Perhaps he was like me in the respect that he viewed himself, through the passage of time, as a series of strangers, some likable, some not. But I must not be presumptuous.

It was apparent, however, that because the accident might really have been an accident, as opposed to a planned occurrence predestined by the machinations of fate, Aldous had become destabilized, not merely physically, but also spiritually. After all, there is no one on earth quite as deranged as a doubting fatalist, and a lapsed fatalist hardly dares to get out of bed to visit the bathroom.

In telling himself this, was not Aldous realizing that, in having doubts about his destiny, he was actually opening himself up to any number of possibilities, so that each act, each step taken, forward, backward, or sideways, represented a decision, as opposed to a certainty? Can we be sure that this realization had come to him, as it must come to us all, sooner or later? Most experience it as soon as they are able to walk or swing a baseball bat, but as I have intimated, Aldous was exceptional and therefore not necessarily subject to the same laws as the rest of us. This is mostly due to the fact that he was orphaned at puberty, the sad butt of Oscar Wilde's quip on carelessness, but it also has to do with the way in which he was brought up; my father always used to say to me, "Be careful, Lenny! Aldo is different from other children!" But he never explained why. Perhaps that's another reason he fascinated me so.

We have said that his father was Italian and his mother American. One catholic, one atheist. One devout, the other empirical. From them Aldous had inherited, inadvertently (which is to say, genetically) a kind of neutrality; it was as if he had been born with his arms stretched out, like a referee, keeping two sides apart. The luck with which he had been born — his temperament (implacable) and his condition (comfortable) — had lent him an insouciance that often displayed itself as naiveté, but that was essentially just a means of getting by, albeit abstractedly. He was not naive. Neither was he ignorant, despite his reserved, deferential air. Of above-average intelligence, he had excelled at school in Latin, Greek, and mathematics. This helped him to deal with life on intellectual grounds; it was the sine qua non for a secular age, but it also helped him spiritually, because he could always resort to literal definitions when dealing with unknown questions and answers. Does God exist? "In Greek times, there were many gods," Aldous would answer, "Zeus, Aphrodite, etc."

Conventional wisdom, conventional faith (or lack of it). These were the things that sustained him throughout his twenties, while he flitted about the globe, staying in hotels for the most part, telephoning friends of friends and sitting on terraces, reading novels. "I have no friends, only friends of friends," he once wrote. To a friend.

The doctor was looking at the X-ray. He looked at the X-ray. Then he looked at Aldous. Then he looked at the X-ray again as if, in some way, there were a similarity between the two, when it was patently obvious that none existed, that one represented the inside, and one the outside, of matter. Clipping the black, shiny plate onto a light box in front of him, he turned to the patient and stared in a manner that would have been vacant, had he not felt the first pangs of lunchtime hunger.

"The particle of dust?" asked Aldous, querulously.

"The particle?"

"Yes. Of dust."

"Dust?"

"Yes. De la poussière."

"But I can't see any dust," said the doctor, turning back to the light box.

He couldn't see any dust! Even Rosalia, old, half-blind Rosalia, could have seen the dust, from the other side of the kitchen!

"But surely you can see it, doctor? It's behind the left eye socket."

"Wait a moment, Monsieur. I'll put on my other glasses. Yes, that's better. Now then, let's see, a particle of dust. A hair, of course, that would be different . . ."

"A hair? What do you mean, a hair?"

"A hair. That would be different. Only yesterday I had a patient with what seemed at first to be a hairline fracture of the skull; but it turned out to be just a line of hair, I mean, quite literally that, a hair caught in the plate."

"But what about mine? Can you see the speck?"

"Ah."

"You can?"

"Yes. There, behind the left eye socket. Of course," he continued, smiling. "The only question is, is the speck on the inside or the outside?"

karma

I awake at dawn with a wooden face (as the French describe it), and as I always do upon awakening to a new day, wherever I happen to be, I consider the various options open to me. Like a huge lily revealing itself after a tropical downpour, myriad virgin petals, each holding the power of the miraculous in its grasp and, along with it, an infinite number of personifications, offer themselves up to me for consideration.

Before leaving Paris, I managed to get hold of a how-to book on Hinduism, in the series Getting Acquainted with the Alternatives (Setter Books, Barksville, Mass.), and I have been quite captivated by the potential of reincarnation. I don't really understand it, of course, but I was greatly encouraged by a Hindu gentleman next to whom I sat on the airplane, who confessed to not really understanding it, either. A Christian will explain his religion by describing the Holy Trinity and the concept of Jesus Christ, a carpenter, who came to the world as the Son of God and who was crucified in order to save our souls, before being resurrected, whereas a Hindu will look at you suspiciously before spending up to an hour trying to explain the word *karma*. But I must be careful here; a fellow scribbler nearly tapped his last after alluding to such matters in one of his more provocative verses.

the aldous and azadina

Returning to the apartment after his doctor's appointment, Aldous Radice was dejected. Further tests would have to be made before it could be determined whether or not "the dust was on the inside." More X-rays would have to be taken. He would just have to wait. Naturally, there was no cause for alarm.

Opening the refrigerator door, he was dismayed to find nothing to eat or drink. He was sure he had put half a dozen Diet Cokes there the day before. Was he imagining things? He certainly could not have drunk them, for he never touched soft drinks. He must be suffering from nerves. He would take a pill and lie down for a while.

Since landing in France, he had made a point of ensuring that there was always at least one can of Diet Coke in the refrigerator, in case Azadina came to the apartment. He hadn't seen her for ten years, but he would never be able to forgive himself if he had nothing to offer her, should they chance upon each other and return to the apartment for a drink. He wasn't exactly sure whether Azadina even liked Diet Coke, but he had seen so many people drinking it lately that he had decided to stock it as a contingency. He couldn't quite remember whether Azadina was a teetotaler or not; he had racked his brains, thinking back to that series of evenings that constituted their affair without being able to put a name to her favorite tipple. To be on the safe side, he had bought an entire cocktail cabinet from the store on the rue de Buci, a stock of alcohol that would cater to the most exotic taste. Every evening since his arrival, he had experimented with the aid of a manual he had procured in New York, entitled *Four Fingers*, and he was so proficient now at making cocktails that he could mix them in his sleep. He had even invented a special loving cup, which he had christened the Aldous and Azadina, a subtle mixture of fresh peach juice, calvados, and champagne, which he planned on having ready at the moment of proposal. But he was nothing if not a pragmatist in such matters, so he would be sure to buy a case of Diet Coke the next morning.

Reclining on the chaise longue in the bedroom, Aldous allowed the calming effect of the pill he had taken to relax his body, from the toes upwards, until he could feel a soft wave breaking gently over his troubled, dusty head.

The window above him reveals to us a view of the Seine; the gargantuan, increasingly noble extensions of the Louvre; upriver to the Pont Neuf, chilly waters dividing neatly, before being reunited at its ancient piers; and downriver, following the racing current, to the Petit Palais and the Grand Palais. And (we must excuse ourselves, opening the window as quietly as we can and craning our necks into the still, August air) to the left the Eiffel Tower, hallmark of the city, reproduced all over the world in the shape of countless objects, which is strange, because the original, being conceived without function, can now be seen to have transformed itself for more domestic use: a ring for keys, an eraser, a base for a bedside light which, illuminated, helps people to read or survey each other's features as they make love, back home.

In sleep, the dust is always on the inside. Everything is on the inside. Aldous will not be able to remember what he is dreaming below the Paris window, but while these dreams are happening, he lives them, enduring their blessings as well as their maledictions, defending himself when necessary against all odds, or swimming along cool, reflective streams, allowing himself to be swept along the current, so that his legs, for some reason, become fins, all the better for navigation and customs clearance.

Things become personified in sleep, and people revert to ideas, representations, misrepresentations, narrative ploys. There are no symbols. A bed is a bed, a book a book, a painting of a book a painting of a book. How many deftless painters have arisen from their slumber, brush in hand, inspired by a dream they might have misconstrued; how many budding warriors have set out, their enemy already sighted, only to find that the penis they glimpsed in their fourth, paradoxical slumber was not a sword at all, but just a penis? No, there can be no symbols, I'm afraid, there is simply no room for them in the busy apartments of sleep. And it is precisely because dreams *cannot* be explained, and not because they can, that makes them so interesting, so powerful, so uplifting.

vishnu

I dream of Paris a good deal here in Tamarama. My dreams are vivid and full of effects;
I can hear them in the form of subconscious
chitchat, while writing about Aldous. I must
be careful, lest they influence my work.

My mind is a painted room and on its
walls are the exquisite renderings of my sleep.
We are particularly impressed with the portraits of our ancestors, a long line of Radishes
stretching back to the founding of Rome, and
the ornithological variations, of which the por-
trayal of two swallows flirting over a birdbath
seems the most prescient.

In one dream, I encounter a Hindu, a
member of the Jain sect, called Bolu, who
takes infinite pains to ensure that no harm is
done to any living creature. It is for this reason that he wears a silk kerchief over his
mouth. Yes, even the incidental capture of a fly
would discredit him! I do not wish to interfere
with Bolu's religion, but I ask him to remove

the kerchief while talking to me, for the simple reason that I cannot hear what he is saying. He complies with my request, but unfortunately, at the very moment that he does so, a wasp appears, as if from nowhere, and flies into his mouth, killing him.

In another dream, I acquire an interesting pet, a crocodile, whom I christen Vishnu. This is a sacrilege, of course, because a crocodile is never cited as a Vishnu incarnation. Referring to my book, I can only find the fish, the tortoise, the lion, the horse, and the dwarf. Yet I have called the crocodile Vishnu, apparently because I consider him to be my preserver.

Vishnu is shortsighted — practically blind, in fact. He came up from a lake nearby and I felt sorry for him. I decide to take him for a walk, a little constitutional, so, after giving him a platter of lamb curry, I clip a retractable lead around his neck and head out onto the street.

The French are libertarians, which is one of the reasons why they are so unpleasant to one another. But they are very accommodating and are known to be most sympathetic toward writers. They are not necessarily proud of their capital, of its gray, linear beauties, rather do they see it, without the slightest trace of arrogance, as a fitting backdrop for their collective genius. The idea that no man is an island is anathema to them, for their nation can be said to be an archipelago composed of a million rocky inlets, all inviting shipwreck if negotiated without due care and attention.

Their attitude toward me has always been one of tolerance, born of incomprehension and respect, a combination which lends the subject room to breathe and move about with impunity. Had I come from the moon, my treatment at their hands could not have been more welcoming; that I come from Brooklyn makes it all the more apposite.

As I walk up the rue de Tournon, on my way to the Sénat, I am impressed by the fact that no one is offended by my pet. There is no lack of curiosity, however.

"Il est très beau, votre chien, Monsieur," says an old lady, with an obliging smile. "De quelle race est-il, si je puis me permettre de vous demander?"

"It's a crocodile, Madame."

"Really? How interesting! We had one, not dissimilar. But that was before the war, of course."

azadina

Azadina is Egyptian. She has no brothers or sisters. In fact, she is quite unique.

The skin of Azadina is brown, but not the kind of brown you might imagine, shifting your gaze from one color sample to the next until the appropriate shade comes to you. It is certainly not "coffee-colored," neither is it mahogany; it is not terra cotta, nor ocher, nor Mars violet, nor burnt nor raw umber, nor Van Dyke brown, nor yellow brown, neither is it English red, or copper, or even, although we are getting nearer, warmer, burnt sienna. Yes, burnt sienna is not a million sand dunes away from the color of Azadina's skin, although, for the purposes of this novel, we shall settle for "light brown," a glistening yet at the same time dryish brown hue, the kind of brown that van Gogh would have traversed the Sahara for, from west to east, or at least walked miles for, from one side of Saint-Rémy-de-Provence to the other, to the art supply shop, once bar, now museum, which one can visit, at one's leisure, to compare the matter that surrounded him to the painting which sprang, like magic, from it. The brown of Azadina's skin is, in fact, somewhere between the 14 or 15 shades of brown that Vincent used on the second book up, right middle foreground, in his painting *stilleven met boeken*. And if we look carefully enough (perhaps there is a magnifying glass in the house somewhere, hiding under a pile of old newspapers) we can see, we can *just* see, the title, in another shade of brown, only one degree darker than the cover, printed on the binding.

Azadina, of course, is both real and illusory, as all lovers are who appear and then disappear in one's life. She lives beyond time, in that space reserved for her in the hearts and minds of countless men, young and old, who have seen her, perhaps only briefly, entering and exiting the Métro at Maubert Mutualité or rubbing shoulders in a windswept line leading to *Zorba the Greek*.

Aldous fell in love with her at first sight, or rather, before first sight, for had not his sixth sense brought them together? No one can really say what the sixth sense is; for some it is intuition, for others telepathy, for still others a convenient aid in going about their daily lives, wondering what to wear or how to organize a dinner party.

The visitor from overseas, the friend of a friend of a friend, is a vegetarian. How fortunate that we should have bought half a dozen free-range eggs earlier, even though we confess to hardly ever eating them! We consider, in retrospect, the divine nature of our acts; we construct from banality, magic, from the superficial, the miraculous! For the most part secular beings, we invest our lives with godly attributes. Witness the lighting of a candle, the flickering ray of hope, the not necessarily coincidental increment to our salary. Karma indeed!

Such a meeting was this! Aldous, visiting Paris in August 1981, installed himself in a swanky hotel on the Right Bank. It was college vacation, his fellow students all seemed to have made plans for sojourns abroad, so he, studying languages ancient and modern, elected to brush up on his French. But with whom, exactly?

After two or three days of languishing in his suite, Aldo chanced upon a telephone number, written in haste on the flyleaf of the novel he happened to be reading, the very one he had started when he met his aunt, my mother, at the Plaza Hotel in New York, one week earlier. Above the scribbled coordinates, the name Leonard Radice, who was, of course, me, resident in Paris for one year as part of a "creative writing program," which is not, contrary to what you might think, a television documentary on graphology, but rather a means to an end, an inversely proportionate equation between technique and imagination, in which the former is always treated as having greater value. (It might not surprise you to learn that *this* particular student did not stay the course, although he did stay in Paris for ten years.)

Leonard Radice was delighted to meet his cousin at the Café de Flore at six o'clock that evening. I was also disappointed, for my cousin never showed up. Well, he did show up, punctually, not at the Café de Flore, however, but at the Café Delors, a more modest establishment on the rue Saint-André-des-Arts.

We both sat, patiently, impatiently. I hadn't seen Aldous for five or six years, and I spent my time wondering whether I would recognize him. After half an hour of waiting, I accosted a tall, thin stranger who, naturally enough, turned out to be just that. He looked embarrassed as I grabbed him by the shoulders and bellowed my prepared welcome, interrupting me at the point at which I beckoned to the waiter for a glass of champagne. His exit was prompt, and I was left alone for a further 30 minutes before deciding to leave. I knew Aldo was a dreamer; perhaps he was sitting in another café, by mistake.

Aldous found the Café de Flore only one minute after I left it. He too had been musing on the problem and had deduced, with the aid of his bar-hopping guide, that there could have been some grounds for a cock-up. Being of an even more pronounced abstraction than myself, he had not reacted favorably to the same problem which had faced me for the previous hour. His survey of the noisy, clattering tables was hurried, for he had already decided to return to the first café, the Café Delors, thinking, perhaps, that I might have arrived there, and then left, during his absence. Slightly exasperated, he retraced his steps, still thinking there was a chance of meeting me.

I was not there, nor was anyone else, save a young woman drinking coffee at the counter. Aldo went up to her and cleared his throat, as he always did upon talking to strangers. She did not turn to face him at this cue. He cleared his throat again and then tapped her on the shoulder. Yes! He touched her! Even before his first glimpse of her light brown face!

The *patron*, drying a glass repeatedly, rubbing its smooth contours with an old cloth before holding it up to the light for inspection, raised his eyebrows for a moment, as if wishing to promote himself to greater significance in our fable. His presence was certainly not gratuitous, however, for by raising his eyebrows a second time, in the direction of Azadina, he encouraged her to break the spell of her thoughts and turn toward the interloper, the now perspiring Aldous.

Not having said anything, it was hard for him to be rendered speechless; this only became evident when he tried to say something, for no words emanated from his nervous lips. Instead, he continued to clear his throat.

"Is something the matter?" were Azadina's first words, translated into French, which now appeared as an arrowed bubble in the space between them.

"Yes. I was wondering whether you might have encountered someone, a creative writer by the name of Leonard Radish?"

"Leonard Radish? Has he been edited in France?" asked Azadina.

"I mean, have you seen such a person here, in this café by any chance?"

"No, Monsieur, I haven't."

"You haven't seen someone who might have looked like him, then?" insisted Aldous, not noticing, perhaps, the quizzical expression that had spread across Azadina's features as she turned back, for a moment, to the counter and her coffee.

azadina's period

Ten years later, possibly to the day (anniversaries are always providential), Aldous awoke with a start, still reeling from the effects of the palliative he had taken three hours earlier and from the dream that had so nearly drowned him. There was blood on the sheet. Azadina must be having her period, he thought. He turned to face her. She wasn't there. Where was she? Aldous was perplexed for a moment. He had been dreaming about her again. A whole decade of Augusts had passed and yet he still dreamed of her, about her, in her.

He sighed. He did not really wish to rejoin the real world, whatever that was. His newly found iconoclasm toward fate was beginning to consume him, as he feared it might. It wasn't simply the "accident" and the dust on the X-ray, which might have been inside or outside his head, there was also the apparent impossibility of ever finding Azadina again, of holding her hand in the rain somewhere, anywhere; he felt trapped all of a sudden, caught in an ever deepening stasis.

He turned to one side and stared at the pile of books on his bedside table, all read, all forgotten, banished to that part of his mind that somehow had a mind all of its own; this was the capricious side, the subconscious side, only it could sum up the real meaning of the books' contents. He tilted his head and reviewed the titles: an encyclopedia, a new one, in French, still cased in its shiny plastic; a doctoral thesis on evolution, written by his friend, Hilton, whose friend had lent him the apartment; an anthology of cousin Leonard's verse, entitled *Ends, Beginnings, Middles*; and, above it, *Le Rouge et le noir*.

Lenny, where was Lenny? What was wrong with his telephone? It sounded like he hadn't paid his bill, or something. "The line was interrupted"; was that a euphemism for insolvency?

Aldous got out of bed, wrestled for a moment with the tartan sleeves of his bathrobe, and made his way into the bathroom. The mirror greeted him with a smile, then a grimace. He looked at his hand; it had blood on it. And then he realized. He had had a nosebleed.

He lathered his face and then shaved, distractedly, so that he cut himself, twice, on the chin. Was he going mad, and if so, what blessings, as Socrates had promised, would come from his madness? Nothing made any sense. He had come back to Paris, chasing his shadow, chasing the shadow of Azadina, which always slipped past him, or underneath him, whenever he thought he had it in his grasp.

There he stood. Frozen, immobile. "The lapsed fatalist hardly dares to get out of bed and take a shower." It must be true. He stared at his face. How strange was the color of blood! It was never quite the right shade.

"I told Azadina," he said, to himself, "that every time we made love it was a new experience, set apart from the other times in the past, in the future, and the more I think about it, the more I feel that *everything* is always new, different, no matter how many times it is repeated, it's part of a never-ending cycle which repeats itself ad infinitum, but always differently. And I know that if the same thing were to happen, in exactly the same way, then I would really go mad. But isn't that what I am trying to do, awake, asleep, isn't that all I really want, to repeat, *exactly*, what happened before, in Paris, in August 1981? The madness doesn't come from wanting. It comes from believing it can happen again."

professional deformation

Writers, like everyone else, are subject to a
certain "professional deformation." The architect sees an architrave and not the face of the
beautiful woman standing below it; the den-
tist, upon meeting his future son-in-law for
the first time, registers the man's nervous
smile with consternation, for there is an apparent need for regular flossing; and the florist,
invited for tea and scones in the sumptuous
apartment of a relative, concentrates his attention on the unusual pastel hue of the birds of
paradise, rather than on the Ming dynasty vase
that houses them.

My deformation takes the form of an
obliqueness toward life that borders on the ex-
istential. This quality has become exaggerated
since leaving Europe for Australia, but it was
always there, influencing me, sometimes without my knowing it. It is inextricably linked to
my profession. Writers are a callous breed; everything that surrounds them is grist for their

mill, subject matter to be used whenever necessary. And that includes Aldous and Azadina, of course.

There are mitigating elements, however, to the megalomania of scribblers. I am not one of those, for example, who believes that everything is possessed of meaning (I have already alluded to my aversion to symbolism); rather do I believe that if meaning exists, then it must spring from action and not the other way around. It is for this reason that true love, when it occurs, is a fact of great profundity and never a sexual diversion. Action speaks louder than words, but you will not be able to convince me that lust ever leads to anything other than transitory infatuation.

Aldous was aware of all this, without acknowledging it. He was certainly a romantic, at least more romantic than most. Throughout his life, action had never been a priority, and up until his return to Paris, there had not been much meaning attached to anything. The questioning he underwent regarding fatalism was ironic, for, in eschewing predestination, he was accepting the arbitrary, the uncalled for, the involuntary in his life. But this had already been confirmed ten years earlier when, by failing to meet his cousin, myself, he had encountered the love of his life. Perhaps he had been too young at the time to realize it, to see that had he not dialed my number, he would have had a completely different adulthood. Now that he was older he was beginning to realize that the way forward, the path to his destiny, was not so much a question of straight on, but left at the lights, right, right again. And then left.

<hr>

Still Life with Books is a love story, and all love stories have good beginnings. The middle, or in-betweenness, varies enormously, depending on the place, the personae, the time of day, and the position of the observer.

Startled to find Aldo getting up to leave halfway through the first act, my father, who had reluctantly taken us on a Broadway outing, whispered angrily into the ear of his spindly nephew. "Aldo! You can't just get up and leave! Sit down!"

Aldous explained that he knew exactly how it would end, that it was therefore uninteresting. I protested: "Hey, Aldo. No one can be sure what will happen. No one can be even sure of what *has* happened. All that we know is in the present, and the present always holds countless possibilities in its grasp."

"Sit down!" hissed my father. "I brought you here to enjoy yourselves, not to have a nervous breakdown. You know damned well I could have been at the track today."

azadina's beauty

The more I think about it, the more I realize that Azadina's beauty is inexplicable, ill defined. It is ill defined because no matter where or how you look at her, she is beautiful, and the beauty that is a part of her expresses itself differently depending on where you happen to be. It is said that beauty is in the eye of the beholder. This is nonsense; it is only the *reaction* to beauty that belongs to the beholder. Aldous and I had a different idea as to the beauty of Azadina. He certainly had more time to consider it, for they shared that hotel suite for two weeks, the last half of that first August, ten years ago. I made love to her once, after Aldous returned to the U.S., at the beginning of September. I know I shouldn't have. But I did.

As far as Aldous was concerned, the myriad points of perspective for assessing the beauty of Azadina all led him to the same conclusion: unequivocal perfection, proven empirically; no matter where he happened to be, whether he was one mile or one millimeter from her, he could say that she was beauty incarnate, a paradigm. But, of course, he could have been exaggerating a little. Love makes us look kindly on matter, its tinted lens comes with the warning, "Objects may appear closer in the mirror than in real life."

Azadina, the figment of an imagination run riot, was at that very moment skipping along an empty boulevard, living proof that beauty is not in the eye of the beholder, for the simple reason that it was so early in the morning that there were no beholders to behold it. She was making her way homeward. Where, precisely, was home? Above the sea and the sky, in that pantheon of deities, nymphs, and dainty spirits whose magic spells invest us merely mortals with the power and inspiration to greatness? Further up and over, in the nether-beyond, to the love nests of celestial, doting cherubs who, at this very moment, as the first rays of a benevolent sun kiss the early morning dew, do dance about, fondling each other, licking lips and making certain suggestions?

No. Home is where the heart is and her heart lived in a sixth-floor walk-up on the rue des Beaux-Arts, not five minutes' walk from the apartment, lent to Aldous by Hilton's friend.

azadina's tail

If we are a product of evolution, mused Aldous, putting down Hilton's doctoral thesis,
then we must, logically speaking, still be
evolving. But into what?

Aldous could not help agreeing with
Hilton. Homo sapiens, such as it was, was
overdeveloped: it no longer required evolving. Put another way, if evolution, like
invention, is born of necessity, what possible
needs could be cited to justify any further
change in our makeup? Did we even need
the evolutionary gadgets at our disposal? The
hands, for example, are far too sophisticated
for most tasks, if one were to discount con-
cert piano playing and brain surgery. In most
cases, such as making love to Azadina, a paw
would have been quite adequate, a reflection
that said perhaps less about Aldo's lovemak-
ing than his dexterity.

What was certain was that, whereas man
had once needed cutlery, it now appeared that

the hand, or claw, was all that was required. The McDonald's near the Luxembourg Palace was living proof of man's change in eating habits, the former a brightly colored clearinghouse for the packaging and unpackaging of bits of fresh plastic and meat; the latter, the crowning glory of a Médici who, tired of the Louvre, removed herself to the Latin Quarter, where she concentrated on her garden and the introduction of the fork. What difference that made to anything was not clear to Aldous, but when wandering around the palace gardens, as was his occasional wont, he couldn't help feeling that the potential for articulation in his legs was never, nor ever would be, fully exploited during any given day's activities.

"Let's pretend we have paws, not hands," he had said to Azadina, once they had crossed the threshold to the gilt and velvety interiors of his hotel suite all those years ago. Or was it somewhere else, on the bench in the rue Saint-Denis perhaps, where they had made love for the first time?

"But I have a tail, Aldo. Haven't you noticed it, yet?"

And it was true. Azadina did have a tail. It was long and thin and dry to the touch, despite its snakelike appearance, which should have made it dry, anyway, for despite appearances there is nothing as dry as snakeskin.

"So you have, Azadina! So you have!"

Well, he could have dreamed it all up, of course.

The bench on the rue Saint-Denis, as we shall discover, is apocryphal. People say that we live in a small world; I cannot tell you how many benches there are, littered about the streets of Paris, some used, some ignored, others bearing the initials of hoodlums, hooligans, or lovers. But I do know that this particular bench was blessed with the spell of providence, for it was on this very bench that Aldo Radice was conceived, in August 1959.

The young Salvatore had traveled by overnight train from Milan to see the sights. Helen Andrews had come to Paris by ship to Le Havre, then by train, and was spending six weeks studying French and indulging in a little *vie de bohème*. Her turned-up blue jeans and beret identified her as an habituée of the Left Bank; in fact, I recently saw a picture of my late aunt, in a monograph of the period, standing behind a street guitarist. The caption read: "Young people gather in order to 'do their thing'."

The two were quite different, but they were in Paris at the same time, so it could be said later that their meeting had been coincidental — sufficient reason, in other words, for them to fall in love. They first met on the steps of the Théâtre de l'Odéon. Neither of them had enough money to buy tickets for the Polish repertory production of *Romeo i Julia*, which, in any case, was sold out. Alone, their predicament depressed them; together, it seemed amusing. They did not need to know that they would spend the rest of their lives together, that they would not, like the couple whose names appeared in neon above their heads, kill themselves, but would die, nevertheless, at the same time, 13 years later. If we all knew what lay in store for us, we would perhaps find it harder to lose ourselves in the moment. *That* moment in 1959, on the steps, was a delight.

Aldo was drawn toward the bench for reasons he would never fully understand. It just seemed like a good place for kissing, a particularly vacant spot, situated between the rue Rambuteau and the rue Étienne Marcel, at the perimeter of the vast site of development known as Les Halles. People passed at a distinctive pace along this street, scurrying back and forth, disappearing into shops that displayed unexpurgated magazines and inflatable women. Some did stand around for a moment or two, but never long enough to consider the bench. There seemed to be too much to do, somehow.

They had dined, following their meeting in the quarter. It was late. Spying the bench with a certain twinkle in his eye, Aldous invited Azadina to join him on its green, rather unforgiving contours. He put his arm around her. They kissed. He told her that she was beautiful, which made her laugh, because he used the formal *vous*, rather than *tu*. A little prematch nerves, perhaps.

Azadina suggested that "beauty was in the eye of the boulder," a courageous attempt at the idiom that did not go unappreciated. Her French and her Arabic were beyond reproach, but her English was culled largely from her attempts to read *The Life and Opinions of Tristram Shandy, Gentleman*. How many hours had she spent only partially deciphering the capricious irregularities of that bastard tongue, immortalized by the eccentric Sterne? Though. Through. Bough. Trough.

There was hardly anyone about at this hour, certainly compared to the earlier part of the evening — just one or two tourists, followed by the occasional couple, their pace slowed by love and wine as they passed Aldous and Azadina, seated compromisingly on the bench. Above them, music could be heard; a party was in progress. They looked up. A row of faces shone in the moonlight, laughing, leaning over the cast-iron balcony that jutted out from the apartment building. Behind them, the soft, gray-leaded rooftops spread upward, cut off by a great expanse of thick, blue night sky. Aldous had Azadina on his lap, facing him, he had

managed to position her with great skill and was
kissing her neck again and again.

"Aldo! We cannot! We cannot! Pas ici!"

But Aldous could. He already had his paws inside Azadina's cashmere sweater, the sensation was
quite exquisite, he was caressing her dark nipples
and pecking at an earlobe while he did so. Time,
place, and the impromptu audience all fell away,
but details in a larger picture filled his mind, an
erotic portrait of an Egyptian beauty whom he now
happened to be holding in his hands.

small mercies

Aldous lost his virginity to a 230-pound opera singer named Heather Small. He made me promise not to tell anyone, but he's dead now. He was 17 years old. Maybe I shouldn't go into it?

He was a natural linguist; he had gone to Europe to perfect his German. My father, in loco parentis, had suggested it and had supplied the funds from the Trust, drawing $1,000 from the bank for the purpose, of which $900 was given to Aldous and $100 put aside for his own incidental expenses (a promising outsider which fell at the last hurdle).

It was another summer vacation. Aldous had flown to London, where he spent two days wandering up and down the King's Road, staring at punk rockers and sitting in cafés drinking ersatz coffee. He took the boat-train from Victoria and traveled across Europe in the dead of night, third-class. It is a journey many have taken but will never take again, at least not in the same fashion, now that the Wall has crumbled and Berlin is just Berlin again, neither West nor East, nor anything in particular.

Arriving at Bahnhof Zoo in the damp rattling dawn, it occurred to the dreamy youth, half lost in the fictional diversions of *Berlin Alexanderplatz* and *Mary*, that he should get practical. He stowed the twin paperbacks inside the zippered compartment of his carryall, the former's cracked spine enveloping the thinner volume and holding it lightly in its grip, so that the fictional strangers within became, for the last phase of the journey, part of the same story.

Summarily directed, in a language he had hitherto only seen chalked upon a board, or heard intoned, cryptically, through plastic headphones, to an agency purporting to deal with such matters as board and lodging, Aldo, having outlined his requirements, was given a piece of squared paper with a name and address printed neatly on it. He took the bus, as suggested, to Bleibtreustrasse (Stay-True Street) checked the number of the apartment building against the now crumpled and slightly moist piece of paper (more nerves), and walked up the three flights of stairs, to the door inscribed SMALL in large, golden letters.

"You must be Aldous. Is something the matter?" came a deep, yet faintly feminine voice from behind his back (he had turned to admire the deco ceiling).

The apartment into which he was ushered was full of operatic properties, trunks, shields, spears, and other miscellanea plucked from the repertory of operas, minor and major, that constituted Miss Small's long, if unremarkable, career. In the corner of the drawing room stood the largest piano Aldous had ever seen, and he found himself wondering whether it might have been tailor-made. It had no doubt accompanied many a shrill rehearsal, many an exotic soirée but, for the moment it was mute, its ebony mouth closed, waiting to be spoken to. Miss Small showed the visitor his room and gave him a front door key.

"Please try not to make too much noise, should you come in late. I am a restless sleeper."

That evening, Aldous did, indeed, return late, having made a cursory inspection of the quarter, stopping at bars and cafés and staring at his increasingly tired reflection in a sequence of brightly lit, yet dusty mirrors. The next morning, at 6:15, he was awakened by the simultaneous knock on his door and entrance of his operatic landlady, towering above him in all her small absurdities. The bulging tray of salami, black bread, and coffee hovered perilously for a moment over his head, and above it, two mighty breasts the size of footballs, attached to the bulk of the soprano with the aid of a gargantuan brassiere.

Any magistrate worth his salt would have called it rape. But let us be thankful, for so near to suffocation did the scrawny teenager come that we are lucky to find him alive and well in Paris at all.

the slip

It is extraordinary what some people can do with a small space, but it is almost miraculous what Azadina had done with her modest apartment, for she had managed to transform a garret of 300 square feet into a château rivaling Chenonceaux in grandeur. It was a veritable pleasure dome, a simple studio advertised in a rainswept realtor's window, and the repository for dreams and dreaming for which she had pined for so long. We make our beds and we lie in them. Azadina's bed was fit for a maharaja.

I visited this place only once. It must have been the last day of August 1991, for on that day all three of us were due to travel south, to Provence; Aldous had told me that the flat was bigger on the inside than the outside, and he was right. I had come by on the way to the Gare de Lyon; Aldous answered the door and showed me in. He sat on the bed next to Azadina and held her hand. I sat at a little desk by the door and watched them, as Azadina got up to make some tea and Aldous lit a cigarette, reclining on a pile of embroidered cushions. I had never seen him so content. He had finally discovered himself through his love for Azadina. Forgive me if I stop and light a cigarette myself at this juncture, for I feel a teardrop welling up inside me. You see, my cousin, within 48 hours, would be dead, killed by an errant wasp.

Paris breathes history. It has a certain formality to it, an order in keeping with its past and its impending future, so that the present takes the form of a thin, white line separating the two. Such a division is a tightrope act, and we must always keep our sense of balance in order to stop ourselves from falling this way or the other.

The *mythomane* has very poor balance. Azadina was not necessarily such a person, although she did know that she could hardly go anywhere without running into a friendly ghost or acquaintance. A student of literature when she met Aldous in 1981, she needed only to step out into the street to check motive, style, or intention with one of her chosen subjects. Eighteen years old and freshly arrived in the city, she was a gifted undergraduate who would matriculate without difficulty.

At that time, she lived with student friends,

sharing an apartment near the Jardin des Plantes. It was there that she and I made love, just a few days after Aldo's return to the U.S. and college. In a way, it was ridiculous. Even now, I can't believe I allowed myself to do such a thing, for I knew damn well how besotted Aldo was with her. Ironically, I had wished to help him out, by returning a silk slip that Azadina had left in his hotel suite. I had seen Aldo off from the hotel and promised to deliver the thing to her as soon as I could. Yes, I was doing him a favor, no less!

I arrived on her doorstep late one evening; Azadina asked me whether I was hungry. Her friends were absent, the new semester had not yet started, so we found ourselves alone. It was the first time we had ever been alone together; I had met her perhaps two or three times previously, but always with Aldo. I went out to the store to buy a bottle of wine and we drank it over dinner. Aldous had told me that Azadina didn't drink, so I was surprised when she nodded each time I picked up the bottle. She got quite drunk, and when she invited me into her bedroom, I should have known better. She put on some music; I can't remember whether it was a tape or a radio station, but what I do remember is her asking me what I thought of her slip. I said it was a nice slip, as slips went. Before I knew what was happening, she had taken all her clothes off and was dancing around the room, singing in Arabic and waving the slip in her hand, above her head. I made a halfhearted attempt to leave at that point. I knew that she wasn't trying to seduce me, that she was just drunk and didn't know what she was doing. I'm not vain enough to intimate that any woman would try to seduce me. But I was younger then, we were all younger, a whole decade younger, and I've told you that sometimes I fail to recognize the person, the people I was, in my past. Whoever that person was, he got laid that night, to use the college vernacular. So perhaps we should blame him.

I don't know how long Azadina stayed in that apartment or when she acquired the one on the rue des Beaux-Arts. I knew that it was her intention to stay in Paris and become a teacher and that she was actually quite a serious girl, with ambition. She told me that once a year she visited Egypt, usually at Christmas, that the family would eat outside, in the garden, with its view of a pyramid, so close to the house that it seemed more like a wall, a Tower of Babel, built upward and not to a point, as one sees in picture postcards. Her father was rarely seen; a retired diplomat, he spent his days partially hidden, in a gazebo, smoking kif. It all sounded rather exotic to a "creative writer" from Brooklyn. Perhaps I was more smitten than I realized.

When I left her old apartment near the Jardin des Plantes, I didn't know that I would not see her again until ten years later. What I thought then was that I'd never see her again. Was that because I felt guilty about cuckolding Aldous? Or was it because I thought that she was just a flight of fancy, for both myself and Aldous, that we would both forget about her? I doubt it. I would be lying if I said that I thought Aldous would ever forget about her, for I knew that he was in love. He had told me as much. I can still hear him, taking me into his confidence as we stepped through the revolving doors of the hotel. "I am going to marry Azadina one day. Not yet. Later. I will come back to Paris to propose to her. I am not sure when it will be, but I know she will accept. We will be very happy but I will die, I will be killed somehow, before we get a chance to walk up the aisle and make our vows. You don't believe me, but I know I am right. I understand the workings of fate. Always have."

borges and wilde

Across the rue des Beaux-Arts from Azadina's apartment stood "l'Hôtel" with its freshly painted facade and, on either side of its entrance, two commemorative plaques, one for Oscar Wilde, the other for Jorge Luis Borges, living proof of history's dusty exhalation, proclaiming, as they did, that one had died and one had lived within the building, at one time or another.

These ghosts, twinned forever in the pluperfect, their essence reduced, in part, to a thin layer of dust covering a row of volumes bearing their names, also floated, imperceptibly, above their respective plaques, which were nailed so resolutely to the wall. Elusive presences, they tended to stick together, sometimes hovering, at other times vanishing, as spirits do, leaving no trace whatsoever except, perhaps, for a small rectangle of dirty brick behind their marble memento mori, ignored by the decorators who had passed their way only a season earlier.

Azadina looked at them through her circular window, and at the row of darkened windows that lined the buildings opposite, all hiding other ghosts, people of every size and description, couples, lovers, old ladies with pets, cats, dogs, alligators. And crocodiles. She thought of Oscar Wilde, the bloated genius whose only crime was buggery, and she thought of Borges, who wrote "to ease the passing of time," "le maître de la nouvelle latino-américaine," as she called him, when she taught her rather diffident adolescents on Tuesdays and Fridays. How could she possibly tell Gaston, Gisèle, and the others that she had actually seen them, Borges and Wilde, standing in the street, waiting for the hall porter to let them in after an evening together at the Moulin Rouge, and that every time the hall porter came to the front door he cursed, thinking that they were a pair of drunks, pulling the bell simply to annoy him?

Moving away from the window and lying down on the silken bed, Azadina caught her reflection, in profile, sliding like a shadow across the large mirror that filled the opposite wall, which made of her, for a fleeting moment, the cat goddess, Bastet, the next, some forgotten ancestor whom one can still see underneath a pyramid in Egypt or, closer to home, in a glass case in the Louvre, a woman of impossible, two-dimensional beauty, whose left eye, spread along the side of her face, was highlighted by makeup extracted from alligator droppings, whose chest, bejewelled, was caked with alabaster powder and olive oil and whose legs were seen frontally and not sideways, making one wonder how women might have gone about their business, or at least walked from A to B in those days, a million Augusts ago.

This particular August, 1991, was half over; it was the nineteenth already. Looking around the room, Azadina told herself that time passed too quickly; it made no concessions whatsoever, just rolling on and on. She had found a photograph from ten years ago; she was laughing with Aldous in the Luxembourg Gardens. The image, the memory that gripped her was cropped into a neat square, its shadow falling across her face, cropping it in its turn. She looked with longing into the worn picture, at herself in love in the arms of Aldous, shifting her gaze along the avenue of trees behind them and above, into the tiny patch of blue sky in the distance, seized by a terrible longing for the man who had once appeared in her life and then vanished, leaving the indelible imprint of love upon her heart.

The moon, full, appeared in the circular window but disappeared just as suddenly as she moved her head to one side, back toward the photograph. She felt its presence though; its light flooded the studio, as it so often did, making her think that her home was haunted, as most places in Paris seemed to be, by someone or other, a jealous lover tormented by infidelity, an old woman consumed by a crocodile she was sure had been a dachshund earlier, or *sad* Oscar Wilde opposite, declaring that either he or the floral wallpaper must go.

And who was it who haunted her, but Aldous, the tall, spindly American who had said he had Italian blood in his veins. She smiled, for she remembered looking at the inside of his arms, at the gray-blue lines disappearing up the sleeves of his shirt, to check. She knew two Aldouses, the man who had shared her nineteenth August in 1981 and the other, his namesake, Huxley, whose anthologies formed a part of her miniature library, stuck between Greene and Ionesco, above her head. Aldous! How in love with him she had been! She had even gone to the bookshop on the avenue de l'Opéra after he had left, just so that she could see his name, in print, on a shelf. And those volumes she had bought, layered with a little dust, were all she had, apart from the photograph, to remind her of him. She got up from the bed and plucked *Brave New World* from all the others, sandwiched in a row. She started reading it. Aldous's namesake, in bold type on the cover, was now more real than the original . . . her original.

Whatever had happened to the original, anyway?

discoveries

All of us owe our existence to a chance encounter, two cells colliding in a crowded room
or on a bench, bathed in shadow. Aldous Radice's debt was to a production of *Romeo and
Juliet* and Azadina's was to a *son et lumière* ex-
travaganza beside a pyramid at which her
parents had first met, her father, a little
stoned, mistaking her mother for someone
else, whose name he had forgotten.

   And me? What is my debt? What prece-
dent might have instigated my conception? I
see my father, the incorrigible "Willy," apolo-
gizing to a young brunette on whose pointed
feet he had inadvertently stepped while strain-
ing forward to catch the photo finish of the
Kentucky Derby. They had both backed the
same horse; apologies, profuse, turn to mutual
excitement as the result is finally posted. Cele-
bratory drinks are proposed and consumed,
followed by dinner, followed by sex and then
me. No. I could never imagine my parents

having sex, which is strange, because I am living proof that they did. In fact, they didn't meet at the races. I have a feeling my debt is owed to some form of Italian-American get-together on Mott Street, circa 1955.

Yesterday, I wrote a letter to my parents, alluding to this matter. I asked them to tell me *exactly* how they met. They never went into details with me before. I mentioned my interest in their first encounter when I was in New York last month. I had accompanied Aldo's body, by plane, across the Atlantic, and was naturally in a rather unbalanced state. My father kept patting me on the back and telling me not to "dwell on anything." I think he thinks I have gone crazy or something. My subsequent trip to the antipodes can only have confirmed this view, and it is for this reason, aside from asking him to tell me of his romance with mother, that I have tried to set out how I feel about everything in a letter. I am not sure what my father will make of my discoveries regarding Hinduism. I shall have to wait and see.

If I am part of an endless, futile process of reincarnation, then so is everyone else, surely? Me, Aldous, Azadina, the concierge back in Paris — especially the concierge, for she is the alpha and the omega of every concierge who ever lived, complaining, every morning, about the noise I made with my typewriter and my curses, causing any number of fellow residents to complain of losing precious sleep.

I am wondering what form the reincarnation of Aldous has taken. Only time will tell. I must finish this story first; who knows, perhaps all will be revealed to me, once my task is over. I keep on looking into the painting, *stilleven met boeken met aldous*, searching for clues.

Last night, I was visited by a strange dream. I saw, in the distance, an Indian girl walking toward me. She was dark and mysterious. In her hand she held an iron, the cord hung over her shoulder like a snake. She asked me to lie down, flat on my stomach. Then she proceeded to press my back with the iron, making sure that all the creases were out. She did a good job and I gave her a ten rupee tip. When I awoke, I was in agony. I couldn't get out of bed; so I am writing this lying down.

I remember once, when I was visiting Rio de Janeiro, Uncle Salvatore losing his temper. I suppose he was similar to my father, because he was Latin, slightly irascible, impetuous.

There is always a tendency to read too much into the past. We can never be a product of specific events, notwithstanding justifications for insanity in the witness box; rather does our character stem from the collective, undefined mass of past experience, the details of which, although capable of being highlighted with the aid of hindsight, seem, on their own, to lose, not gain, their value. My uncle's irascible nature, therefore, should not necessarily draw us to the conclusion that Aldous was a "withdrawn, neurotic being, treated sadistically throughout childhood." Psychologists and psychiatrists like to talk of two influences, the genetic and the behavioral. The prosecution prefers to concentrate his attention on the exact movements of the accused at the time he claims to have been "at home watching the '11 O'Clock News.' "

Those past experiences, the holding of a clammy hand, being dispatched to a forgotten corner, the smell of floor wax or pig fat, all the keys to memory, a million, a billion things constituting every conceivable, formative influence placed on us, not to mention the fabled DNA, a veritable hornet's nest of inherited characteristics, are all, inextricably, a part of us, so that it would be literally impossible for me to say that Aldous, Azadina, or I were products of anything in particular; rather of everything in general. We bathe in a great pool of all that we have assumed or collected in our lives making waves, splashing about, displacing, agitating the picture continuously.

Others dive in at their peril.

I remember once playing soccer in the street with Aldous, along with the other urchins from the beach in Rio, and the horrified look on my cousin's face when he heard his father's voice booming at him.

"Aldo! Where are you? Vieni qua! Subito, ragazzo!"

For a moment Aldo just stopped in his tracks and stood there, trembling. Then he ran up to the apartment. I wasn't quite sure what to do, so I followed him. Once we got inside the front door, Aldo looked back at me for a moment before heading off down the hallway toward his father's study. He knocked on the door and went in. I am ashamed to say that I tiptoed down the hall after him and put my ear to the door. I needn't have bothered; I could have heard Uncle Salvatore from the beach.

He was furious. He wanted to know what had happened to his charts of the Amazon. "They've disappeared," he kept on saying. "Have you been playing with them, boy? Well, answer me!"

"No, sir!" mumbled Aldous, under his breath. He was petrified, I could feel it, even with a stout door between us.

"Well, where are they? I'm flying to Manaus tomorrow morning and I need them."

Now I was trembling, for of course I knew where the charts were as well. We had spent the night before studying them, planning trips, magical excursions; we had even drawn a line on one of them, from Barão de Melgaço to Boa Vista, a conquistador's trek annotated with stops for Coke and hamburgers. The worst of it was that it had been my idea; I had persuaded Aldous to go into his father's study and get them while Uncle Salvatore was downtown at a meeting, despite my cousin's protestations. I had even taunted him when he had said that his father would kill him if he messed around with the charts.

"Actually, father," I could hear Aldo saying. "I do know where they are, come to think of it. I was having a look at them in my bedroom last night. I'll go and get them for you."

I moved away from the door at this point, so as not to be seen. But the door didn't open until Aldo had received a good thrashing.

"You lied, Aldo! You lied!" I could hear Uncle Salvatore shouting. "And that's the worst thing you can ever do! I knew you had taken the charts. But you told me you hadn't."

a thinned character

I must disappoint those of you who are possibly still waiting for the appearance of a "rounded character" in this novel, someone similar to the one proposed by the English novelist, the unyielding Bardoch, who once lectured us in college, someone "to really get one's teeth into."

I remember being greatly impressed by that rather lumpy pedagogue's analogies to food and the substance of matter made while declaiming from the podium. I have always considered this obsession with "roundness" to be peculiarly English, a somewhat Hogarthian concept, rooted, as it is, in the tradition of caricature in eighteenth-century Anglo-Saxon art and literature. The funny thing is, old Burdoch, unlike Azadina, had never even read Laurence Sterne. And he an Englishman!

Aldous Radice was probably the nemesis of Mr. Burdoch's fictional hero, or antihero, for he was an ectomorph, a thin, unrounded person, as discussed by another Englishman, Aldous Huxley, in a lecture he gave at Santa Barbara in the late 1950s that Aldo's mother may or may not have attended but certainly knew of, for it is included in the anthology entitled *The Human Situation*, a worn copy of which was to be found in the Radice's Ipanema apartment, which I remember reading, without fully understanding, at the age of 11 years and 7 months. What I do recall is the notion that the physiological and physical attributes of any given character not only mean that he is "round" or "thin" or whatever, but also that he is, for example, "willowy by nature" or "obese in his thinking." I hope the estate of Aldous Huxley will forgive my interpretation; it's been a while since I read the willowy author and I can't find *The Human Situation* here in Tamarama.

As far as my analysis of Aldous Radice is concerned (safer territory), I can say that, certainly up to the "accident," he was a man resolutely stuck in the subjunctive tense, that state in which action is always subordinate to intention. It was only his belief in fate that led him to the Newtonian principle of action and reaction, ensuring that, at critical moments, he "did," rather than "planned on doing." He certainly did not believe in the interpretation of simultaneous events as coincidence. We will discover that he was not in the least surprised at being reunited with Azadina, even though, to us, it seems fortuitous, to put it mildly. I am looking for alternatives in order to find meaning in my life. Aldous did not need to look: a loner, he held all the secrets in the palm of his long, thin hand.

People said of Aldous that he was lazy, lacking in ambition and a "dilettante." Geniuses have suffered worse compliments!

What one does not know cannot hurt one, and, as these observations were made behind his back, it is impossible for me to record how he might have reacted to them. In direct conversation with people who might have been his friends, had they not been just friends of friends, or acquaintances, these perjorative asides would turn, miraculously, into euphemism, so that, instead of being "lazy," he would be accused of "having a ponderous disposition"; instead of "lacking in ambition," he would be censured for "not making full use of his enormous potential"; and instead of being a "dilettante," it would be suggested that he should perhaps "concentrate his considerable intellect in one particular field." My father would always say that he needed a job, but he never specified which. His advice, like all advice of a coercive nature, went in one of Aldo's ears and got lost, somewhere, with all the other dust.

It is easy to see why everyone took to giving

Aldous advice, for in many ways he was a sitting target. People always seem to get what they do not ask for in this life, and the simple fact that he never solicited advice in the first place was ample enough reason for his being given it. The proof of that little equation is that, had he actually asked for it, no one would have been able to say they were in a position to help. Who were *they* to think they knew him well enough? No. The real reason people gave Aldous advice was that he was a complete mystery to them. His very simplicity confused them, upsetting their world projections, so that Greenland appeared even bigger than it should have.

"Simplicity" might have been too hastily selected. Let us say that Aldous Radice was entirely lacking in caprice. He was incapable, after the age of eight, of lying. Furthermore, he had never felt jealousy. A conundrum indeed!

Everyone knows that one of the tricks of memory is size, so that everything becomes smaller in retrospect; the giant of childhood becomes the dwarf, the Tower of Babel, a modest skyscraper, and Heaven turns out to be nothing of the sort, just a big mass of darkness comprised of so many million "light years," the ultimate conundrum, of course, as anyone knows who has tried to find the bathroom switch in the dead of night while drunk. Light or dark, time assumes its own perspective, as clearly as an architect's drawing, its vanishing point never truly vanishing, despite the size of the building, the enormity of the landscape.

Holding his head up to the light in the apartment lent to him by Hilton's friend, Aldo mused on the nature of time, distance, and the surfeit of dust, a particle of which may or may not have lodged itself within his cranium. He was not frightened of death, for death was where his parents lived. It was the unknown that put the fear of God in him.

The image on the radiograph was shadowlike, it resembled some ancient *mappa mundi*, a splendidly naive vision of our celestial home, in which the Old World eclipsed future discoveries so completely that one wondered where they might have disappeared to. The head of Aldous could be turned like a globe, the better to inspect its mysteries, to orient the subject correctly. Fixed in a certain orbit, extended above the living head from which it had been taken, this X-ray, proof of the roundness of matter, seemed somehow to follow Aldous around the room, as an extension of his right arm, and as it did so, it taunted him with the same question: Is the dust a figment of the imagination or does it actually exist, a true object in a true sphere?

the shadow of dust

There Aldous sat, in the armchair that he had
positioned very carefully so he could see people passing along the quai, on both sides of the
street, and, with his binoculars, across the
Seine to the street that ran alongside the
Louvre. He had put the X-ray aside and had,
for the moment at least, cast away those dark
and morbid thoughts, the workings of fate, the
fate of the workings.

The binoculars he had inherited from his
father; they were extremely powerful and effi-
cacious, an indispensable guide in his quest for
Azadina. In fact, they were all he had. He had
telephoned her old apartment, he had telephoned Information, he had telephoned me,
and he had telephoned the Egyptian Embassy.
He had even tried all the primary and secondary schools in Paris; how was he to know that
Azadina commuted to Levallois to work?

Had he known where Azadina's apartment
was located, just two blocks away, toward the

boulevard Saint-Germain, he might have trained his binoculars in a different direction. But although they were powerful, they could not, like X-rays, see through walls, so such an expedient would have rendered him as frustrated as he was now, seeking out Egyptian qualities from the mass of faces that appeared in the Siamese circles in front of him. He put his binoculars down and closed his eyes, applying the lens covers to his eye sockets, like monocles.

It was at this point that the dot appeared. The dot was the particle of dust, or its shadow, which, since the accident, always appeared, sooner or later, when he closed his eyes tightly. If it was a sunny day, the dot would move on an orange background, and if Aldous was lying in darkness, perhaps in that crucial state that is man's prologue to sleep, when sudden escape from morbid thoughts always seems impossible, the background would be gray or black. Today, the background was blue-black, the color of Azadina's hair when it was caught in twilight.

Having appeared from outside the picture frame that was Aldous's inner view of matter, the dot stuck to a certain trajectory, moving in a straight line as surely as if it had been drawn with a ruler. It was up to Aldous to arrest its progress, which he could only succeed in doing if he concentrated hard enough. Even then, when he employed all the powers at his disposal, it was still impossible for him to hold it in place forever; sooner or later it would continue on its way, ultimately disappearing through the opposite side of the picture frame.

When he relaxed his attention for a moment, the dot would then pick up where it left off, as if it had never been interrupted; then it would be only with an almost superhuman effort that he would manage to stop it again. In this way, the dot seemed to be telling him that he had just one chance and that, once he had seized it, he had no real choice but to immobilize it forever. The dot, the shadow of dust, had a mind of its own in this respect. Although it was only an object, a minuscule example of matter on the move, it represented to Aldous an idea, which was the struggle between two elements: *will* and *time*. Time could be stopped, through volition, but it could not be forgotten, put to one side, ignored.

He opened his eyes. Why else have I come back to Paris, he thought, but to prove, through love, that I can arrest time and, by so doing, realize my destiny: to be reunited, however miraculously, with Azadina?

"raising a spirit in his mistress's circle"

Azadina, at that very moment, was in her studio, holding the photograph of herself and Aldous. She was recalling the time she had faked an orgasm for him. It could not have been on *the* bench, for even a faked orgasm would have been difficult there, with everyone passing by, pretending not to look at them, or with the row of heads above, on the balcony, staring down. No. It had been somewhere else. In the hotel.

Aldous had been lying on top of her, talking into her ear, telling her that she was immortal. She was 18; she'd never met anyone quite so serious before. She felt a little uncomfortable, as Aldous made love to her; it would have hurt had it not given her so much pleasure. In fact, it was only later, after she had gotten up the next morning and gone for a walk in the gardens with Aldous, that she had felt any discomfort.

Azadina was completely uninhibited about her sexuality, as I discovered myself, of course, shortly afterward. She had no hang-ups, no axe to grind, no other metaphorical obstructions to being herself. She enjoyed being a woman, and she reveled in her beauty, which gave her an advantage over others. That said, she was aware that women were often treated badly, especially in France, where practically every domestic product advertised on television was accompanied by a nude model tiptoeing across a checkered floor or skipping, inanely, through soft, wooded meadows littered with toilet tissue or bleach. Or yogurt.

Aldous kept repeating to her that she was immortal, pawing at her buttocks and pushing himself into her, harder and harder. She hadn't felt she was really participating in anything at that point, because her mind, her intellect had taken over. It had been offered a problem to solve, and it couldn't deal with it. Immortality? What did immortality mean, exactly? Every 18-year-old was immortal! It wasn't even worth thinking about!

As Aldous felt himself coming, he whispered more things in her ear, which she couldn't understand, partly because her English wasn't good enough and partly because his excitement made his words indecipherable. Usually, she would have come with him; she generally came, many times, during sex. But this time, she couldn't, because she was trying to work out what Aldous was saying. So, she faked it. And, as she faked an orgasm, she *had* an orgasm, which made her wonder, ten years later, whether the counterfeit always led, ultimately, to reality. Like crying wolf.

She put her hand between her legs and called for Aldous. Would he come to her, if she repeated his name long enough?

un romancier créatif

The history of the affair between Aldous and
Azadina, like all such histories, is characterized
by a certain amount of disappointment and
revelation. It only lasted for 14 days, but its
memory lingered, indefinitely. True love never
fails, largely because it ignores the passage of
time.

Azadina took quite easily to the stranger
she met by chance that evening, intrigued by
him more than excited as he stood there, nervously asking questions. She had great curiosity
then, and it was a curiosity that had to be satisfied. She had arrived in Paris at the end of July,
fresh from Cairo. Everything was new to her
and she enjoyed standing in cafés or at bus
stops, watching a foreign world go by.

"You haven't seen someone who might
have looked like him, then?" repeated Aldous,
as Azadina turned her back to him in the Café
Delors. Apart from enquiring as to my where-
abouts (I was doubtless entering the Café de
Flore at that very moment) he was also stalling

for time, rendered motionless by the sight of Azadina. "A creative writer, *un romancier créatif,*
someone holding a pen in his hand, scratching his
brow, pontificating?"

"Un romancier créatif?" The tautology be-
mused her, but only for a second. The sight of the
stranger smiling made her think that perhaps he
was joking. She smiled with him.

"No, Monsieur. I'm afraid I haven't. What is a
'romancier créatif,' anyway? Could he be American
by any chance?"

"Yes. Absolutely. So, you have seen him,
then?"

"No, you don't understand. I haven't. In fact, I
haven't seen anyone enter this café, except you,
since I arrived, five minutes ago."

It was only to be expected that the young Aldous,
having not much else to do, except read novels in
his hotel suite or go for walks in the gardens or
along the river, would return to the Café Delors
every day for the rest of that week and spend a couple of hours there, a period that covered, on either
side, the exact time at which he had returned to the
bar, that evening, to find Azadina standing at the
counter.

He liked the Café Delors, in any case. It had a
charm about it, it was a local, rather than a tourist
spot, or dot. It was his handy bar-hopping guide

that had led him there in the first place (I had never even heard of it, which is why I so easily confused it with the Flore), and he was horrified, one evening, to see two tourists arrive within three minutes of each other, the same guidebook in hand. He averted his gaze, but could not avoid hearing the usual, bleary protocol that always followed such encounters. Washington State, said one. Normal, Illinois, said another. Why did people always ask each other where they came from and not where they were going? It didn't make any sense.

By the time Azadina returned to the historic café (in which, we are informed, various writers and artists were wont to sit, in the 1920s, discussing Botulism), Aldous had become something of a regular. He waited a full 15 seconds before accosting her, tapping her shoulder and smiling. "It's you! Quite a coincidence!"

Azadina was a little wary, yet nevertheless enchanted. "You found the *romancier créatif*, or was it just your imagination?"

He bought her a coffee. The patron raised his eyebrows again; it seemed to Aldous that he did little else. They made a date for the next day. There was an exhibition, somewhere. Or something. It was closed. So they went for a walk and later had dinner. He took her home to the apartment by the Jardin des Plantes and arranged to meet her the following evening. And the next.

sweat

They were lying in bed in the hotel. It was the night they had made love on the fabled bench. They had walked all the way from the rue Saint-Denis to the avenue Georges V, and they were tired. They couldn't sleep, though; they stayed awake until dawn, holding each other, listening to the refuse trucks, telling stories.

"When they first discovered the tomb of Tutankhamen," Azadina said, "they heard strange noises. Perhaps they thought it was the murmuring of the spirit they had disturbed. It wasn't. It was the chemical reaction of the tomb's interior upon being exposed to the desert air, after 3,000 years of being locked up, confined in a small space. That was in 1922; the degradation has continued ever since. Today, millions of tourists pass by; their collective sweat condenses on the walls and workers have to chip off the layer of salt with chisels."

"I would like to go there," said Aldous.

"No. It's too late, Aldo. Those murals, portraits, signs, and symbols, they are all wrecked now. You would be just one more perspiring tourist, stealing the art around you with your presence."

"I could use a deodorant."

"That might help. But in a way it would be worse, for instead of sweat, our ancestors would begin to reek of cheap perfume."

Aldous raised his arm from its place around Azadina's shoulder and sniffed at it. "But it's not cheap, Azadina. It's supposed to be the best money can buy."

"Well, perhaps we could make an exception. My father might be able to arrange a private tour, if he hasn't been smoking too much kif in the garden."

a servant with intuition

The Indian girl who appeared in my dream earlier has returned. She fascinates me. It might sound strange, but I greatly enjoy her ironing of my back. It is an unconventional massage, I admit, but a singularly effective one, nevertheless.

She appears in my sleep, unannounced, whenever she pleases, then leaves, just as mysteriously. It is only after her third or fourth visitation that I realize that she comes not when it pleases *her*, but when she thinks it might please *me*, usually after I have had an exacting day of writing and reminiscence. A servant with intuition!

I think I have fallen a little in love with this dark, snake-eyed beauty. Yesterday, she put her iron aside and gave me the most delicious attentions to my nether regions, making of my member a staff as strong and as stiff as the most defensive cobra; the head was off the ground and the purple beast almost took off at the moment of orgasm.

I am not sure whether it is a question of love or infatuation. I have always had great difficulty in distinguishing between the two. What are words, anyway, but variations, misrepresentations, the blunt chisels of a scribbler! But whatever it is that I feel for her (and by feeling, no words will ever do it justice) I know that it is sufficiently strong for me to have allowed the memory of Azadina to slip a little from its place in the pantheon of female deities at the back of my mind. In transferring my latent affection for her, am I not admitting to the superficial nature of the male sex, always ready to sacrifice itself for the sake of a woman, just as long as another, more beautiful, does not take her place? "Young men's love then lies / Not truly in their hearts, but in their eyes."

But all generalizations are false, are they not?

When I look back, perhaps the strangest thing of all is that during both Augusts, 1981 and 1991, Aldo and I only met by chance. During the first, as I have explained, we missed meeting through the confusion of the Café de Flore with the Café Delors (I will explain later how we eventually bumped into one another), and during the second, it took nearly three weeks before we met, largely because my line had been "interrupted"; yes, they had cut off my telephone. What can I say? I was broke. August in Paris, for a creative writer, is a lean month.

Aldous finally wrote me a note from the quai Voltaire, explaining that he had taken an apartment owned by Hilton's friend and would be staying in Paris for the month of August, but I didn't even get that until after I had returned from a few days' vacation in Brittany. This was only two months ago, but the exact dates escape me. I don't keep a diary, I'm fairly chaotic in daily life, I was incommunicado at the time and had not even spoken to my parents for a couple of months. If I had, my mother would surely have told me that my cousin was coming to Paris and that I should keep a weather eye on him. You can well imagine how she reacted when I called her from Saint-Rémy, at the beginning of September, to tell her that Aldo had been killed by a wasp. Sure, I know my way around France, I lived there for ten years, but was it my fault that that demonic insect flew from the beer glass into Aldo's mouth?

"to beautify him only lacks a cover"

If vanity is a vice, then a hairdressing salon is a veritable den of iniquity. One stares at one's reflection, turning the head a little to this side, or to that, the better to view oneself to one's advantage.

Aldous Radice, a fortnight before he died, was certainly handsome, if one had to put a name to his looks. Like everyone else, he had good features and bad ones and, as is often the case, all depended on the configuration, by which I do not necessarily mean that the nose was situated in the center of the face, between the mouth and the eyes (although this helps) but rather that the ensemble was possessed of a logical, yet intangible allure.

He was fortunate in having features of character in good proportion to each other, dark, brown eyes, which revealed both intelligence and sadness, lips rather thin, yet elegantly so, and a nose of angularity and rectitude that reminded the observer of his Latin blood, bringing to mind a hazy, black and white photograph, taken perhaps in Trieste, in the 1920s (at about the time that Howard Carter first bumped his head on King Tut's tomb) that was not, of course, of Aldous, but of his paternal grandfather, Italo Radice, the entrepreneur and celebrated author, whose face, somewhat similar to Aldo's, had been reproduced in magazines of the period, often causing young society ladies to swoon a little as they encountered it while having their hair attended to, prior to some important function.

This process of assessing one's worth is occasionally hampered by the ministrations of the barber who, after all, is only doing his job. One is nevertheless constrained to stare at oneself, from whatever dubious angle, for a considerable length of time, at least longer than one ever has to under different circumstances. The adjustment of the paisley tie in a restaurant mirror, the verification of a certain jauntiness, caught transitorily in the window of a department store, or the diurnal ablutions that inaugurate the day, none of these things, even in total, can hold a candle, as it were, to the 20 or 30 minutes of sustained consideration that characterize a visit to the hairdresser's. Do we enjoy looking at ourselves, at the series of acquaintances who pop in to see us, all sporting shorter and shorter hair? Are we handsome chaps? Are we attractive to the opposite sex, if indeed that is our intention? Are we going gray, becoming wrinkled, sprouting follicles from the nostril? Or, has Azadina found someone of greater worth, finer hair, ampler genitals?

After three days of self-imposed incarceration, sitting with his shadow in the armchair, Aldous finally quit the apartment and set out to meet his destiny. He would have a haircut, revisit the radiographer, walk around a little, retrace old steps, have a bite to eat.

It occurred to him, while the barber trimmed his hair and shaved his neck, using a cutthroat razor not dissimilar to the one van Gogh used to trim his ear, that the particle of dust in his head might have been some other element, a piece of dandruff perhaps, neglected by some earlier trimming and that, by having his hair washed and cut, it might simply disappear, either swept into the curved sink against which the back of his head rested while Spiros lathered him or dislodged, later, by the barber's fingers, as they massaged his troubled cranium.

"Little tense today, sir?" hazarded the naturalized Cypriot.

"Perhaps."

How extraordinary that the man remembered him from ten years ago.

"Life is good. Yes. Very good," he was saying.

"A little money. Few connections. Import. Export. Good woman, little holiday now and again. Cyprus, Florida. Wherever. Whatever you want. Just 'ave to know what it is. That's all."

Spiros was standing quite still, his razor in the air, a smile on his face. Aldous looked at him in the mirror. The picture was frozen, a portrait of two reflections, which I have plucked from my album for the aid of this story.

After the haircut, Aldo walked over to the rue de Rennes, the radiographer's envelope under his arm. At each intersection, he thought he saw Azadina, waiting with him at the flashing lights, standing at attention, or coming toward him, skipping over the pavement, mouthing the words of a song, two black wires protruding from her ears. Everywhere he went, it was the same story. Flying in from New York, at the beginning of the month, he had been sure he had glimpsed her, in profile, cut out of a cornfield as they had come in to land. Even the landscape looked like her, the detail was there, for all to see, from 5,000 feet! It had startled him. Was it his mind, turning everything he saw into her face, or was it the projection of fate, leading him on, each image a clue, another step in the right direction?

In the doctor's waiting room, he said to himself that this would have to be the last time. He couldn't keep coming back; returning was fast becoming the leitmotiv of his existence. He had to get this "particle of dust" business sorted out before being reunited with Azadina.

In his hand was the X-ray, which he had removed from its envelope, the radiograph of his cranium, the *mappa testa aldiana*, two bent circles, or eclipses, one inner, one outer, constituting a private and a public universe, with all the relevant features carefully noted, global fissures, tributaries, fumaroles, still waters, mountainous ridges and valleys, tectonic junctures, and broad, circular plains, all mirroring, topographically, the restless interiors of his psyche. From his late mother's womb had this object sprung, through her vagina had it passed . . . and there were still bends and dips, curves and dents to prove it.

Alone in the waiting room, time passed unsurely, judged not by the minute hand of a clock, for there was none, but rather by the repeated selection and rejection of periodicals, all of which had been well prostituted since publication, so that their covers had developed creases, arbitrary wrinkles added to the famous, or infamous. Sufficiently abstracted from the iconography of our age not to recognize the key names pasted on the foreheads of the tanned, smiling figures gracing these fading glossies, Aldous could only gaze in bewilderment at them, while waiting to learn of his fate. It seemed that an artist by the name of Pen, or Pin, had not undertaken lightly his decision to have a vasectomy. Elsewhere an equally prominent member of the species, a woman this time, seated in an armchair of the Le Corbusier school, was brave enough to admit that "anybody who enters my life generally ends up in my books." Books? Shouldn't it have been "nooks"?

Still another celebrity, an actor this time, was seen to pronounce the words (in bold type across his highly polished face): "I grew up thinking I would marry the first woman I had sex with," an assertion that made Aldous think of Miss Small. He wondered what might have appeared on this character's X-ray, a little heart, perhaps, in pink, an arrow pointing toward a charming enough nymph, a slip of a thing slithering into stardom, his chosen one, the perfect mate with whom to dance, swim, and "have sex with." What furtive grapplings, the denouement of what sandy tryst might have ensued as a result of this screen idol's childish fantasies! An adolescent erection leaping across the screen of a drive-in movie, mimicking fingers mimicking a rabbit, or a crocodile perhaps, anything designed to be stroked or tickled.

"Míssure Radéesh? Òww ées yōre èd?"

the navel of heaven

I think the term *creative writing* must have been coined by the same person who came up with "creative accountancy." I studied it because I couldn't think of anything else to do when my father packed me off to college. He had spent many afternoons and evenings hustling to finance it, so when I look back, the irony of my doing something I didn't really want to do for someone who couldn't really afford it, does not escape me. And where did it get me? Australia.

According to the Rig-Veda, the fire god, Agni, will consume my body at cremation, before carrying me aloft to heaven. Once ascended, I shall be reunited with Aldous and other members of my family, past and present. Everyone will drink *soma*, the immortal elixir. These will be good times, timeless times. I will apologize to Aldous for causing him to avert his gaze just before he died and for sleeping with his girl. He will forgive me, I'm sure. Oh yes, I shan't forget to mention the time I encouraged him to take the Amazon charts from his father's study.

I will soon learn whether my soul will be excused from further rebirth, whether it will be my destiny to return to the world in human form, or, thirdly, whether I will be condemned to live the life of an insect or a reptile, possibly the crocodile whom I took for a walk in my dream.

Soma is a god of naturalistic origins, a fact which must have appealed to Huxley when he included it in his *Brave New World*. A plant, it is also known by the name of *hoama* in Iran (if you happen to be passing through) and is used in sacrifice. It is a life-giver, the very stuff of immortality. In the early Upanishads and Brāhmanas, a correlation is made between the drinking of this potion and the identification of the human soul with the Absolute. The yellowish juice from this plant is filtered through a sieve and is closely connected with rain, so that Soma becomes the lord of streams and the son of the waters, while its golden color is related to lightning and also to the sun's rays. The filter of the sieve is perceived as the sky, Soma becoming "the navel of heaven in the woollen filter" (Rig-Veda 9.12.4)

A cocktail, in short, with a kick to it, sufficient incentive when consumed in quantity by Indra, the Hindu warrior god, for him to trample on the most valiant enemy. Even imbibed as one part *soma*, three-parts Diet Coke, it is enough to anesthetize anyone from practically anything.

no anomaly

Almost running and yet restraining himself, so that a kind of lilting gambol, or gamble, resulted, Aldous Radice made his way back along the rue de Rennes with no radiograph in his hand, the palm of which no longer sweated, either.

He had thrust the offending object, the pretext for 14 days and nights of morbid introspection, with some glee, into a large green refuse bin and it now lay not so much covered with dust but with the discarded roll and mayonnaise of the lunch of one Frédéric Pilaffe, whose vain attempts to court Marie-Thérèse, the assistant at a nearby fashion outlet, had preempted carpaccio at an adjacent eatery (a table at which he had rashly booked in advance) leading him to a quick hamburger on the sidewalk instead, which actually made him vomit. He felt doubly cheated, as the girl in the television commercial the night before had burst into song after eating hers.

Aldous's hand, now free, brushed its

master's freshly cut hair, which had been caught, momentarily, in an updraft of wind billowing from a Métro grille, as the hero of our tale continued on his way, purposefully, through the traffic of bodies and perambulators.

It seems the particle of dust had never really existed, except in his imagination. A third and final X-ray had revealed a completely dust-free cranium, as surely as if Rosalia had taken the vacuum cleaner to it. If it had ever existed at all, then the little culprit could only have imposed itself during the first X-ray, caught on the plate and subsequently exposed by default. No, there is nothing quite as reassuring, unless you happen to be a hypochondriac, as a doctor's smile: "Il n'y a pas d'anomalie."

Safe in the knowledge that he no longer needed brain surgery, Aldous returned to the apartment, to ready himself for the evening, only troubled by the memory of Uncle Willy, who had once intimated that he was a hypochondriac, when Aldous was 13 and smitten with some ailment, the nature of which escaped him.

He went into the kitchen and prepared himself an Aldous and Azadina, his delicate blend of liquor and peach. Then he sat in the armchair, basking in the glow of his most recent impersonation, that of a free and fit man with the world as his oyster. He looked through the window, at Paris walking by.

How many of those people might be suffering, quite unwittingly, from brain damage, of one sort or another? They were all going home from work, they were tired, they didn't even have time to have their brains examined. And here was he, Aldous Radice, as free as a bird, *dustless!*

An hour later, having satisfied himself that a starched collar and pheasant-feathered bow tie was not overdoing it, he set out to retrace some more steps, this time across the river, to the restaurant where he dined every evening.

His entire disposition toward the city had changed; he could feel it in his bones. He had begun to blame it, the Parisians, the French in general, not only for the entire dust saga, fate's uncharacteristic demonstration of choice in his life, but also for the continued disappearance of Azadina which, of course, was obviously related to all the formative elements of predestination so implicit in his destiny. Yes, the whole lot of them were responsible, collectively, corporately; they had been putting him off track ever since he had slipped in the shower — from the lackadaisical radiographer to the sales staff of the department store opposite, who, exiting the shop three days earlier, had doubtless obscured his view of his beloved. And what about the manufacturer of the shower tiles, the soap, the faulty thermostat? It was a conspiracy!

For this reason, misanthropic qualities had

begun to surface in him; had he not tried, even yesterday, to actually inflict harm on a pigeon, in the place Saint-Sulpice, that of course had not done anything to offend him other than flap nervously about his head, but which he had deemed to have been in cahoots with the rest of his tormentors? And who knows who that pigeon might have been or what it might have symbolized, other than the fleeting impediment to his search for Azadina? But all that didn't matter now. Everything was different. Everything.

A strange disappointment engulfed him, however, as he entered the Cambodian restaurant, a feeling that stemmed from the fact that he had been designated "normal," that he was no longer a special case, separated from everyone else by the persistent proximity of his own mortality, although we cannot discount the possibility of the hypochondriac's chagrin at finding himself in perfect health, if indeed, such an accusation could be laid at his feet. A rather dull and thudding sentiment filled his heart, for whatever reason, a pedestrian feeling in tune with the ponderous steps that carried him forth, across the threshold of the Chung Kock and to the table, reserved for him, as usual, in the corner, beside an aquarium that was filled, incidentally, not with brightly colored tropical fish, as one might have expected, but with empty bottles of rice wine, as it is known in the Orient. This feeling was probably just one of anticlimax, augmented by a distinct vacuity, the result of negation, the arrested obsession of dust on the brain. He brushed it aside.

The waiters were friendly. Wide smiles accompanied bony handshakes, followed by drinks. Aldous had eaten at this spot so often that ordering was no longer necessary; plates and bowls just arrived, as if telepathically.

As the meal progressed, it became increasingly clear that he would have preferred, in a way, to have remained subject to the investigation, now interrupted, of his head, not in the same way of course, although it had to be admitted the dust business had given him a modus vivendi; it had been a theme in his life that, in retrospect, he had rather enjoyed, despite his feelings to the contrary when it had all been happening. It had, after all, set him apart, providing him with a focus for his imagination. He hadn't enjoyed the visits to the radiographer, he didn't see himself as a hypochondriac, nor as a masochist, but he did feel a certain satisfaction at having had the chance to examine his head, of glimpsing the inside. It demystified everything; that great, dark fishbowl of matter was a revelation to him. It was all, ultimately, so simple, so exquisitely simple! He was like a character in a play, a man no longer young enough to be forgiven his foolishness, in love with a girl he hadn't seen for ten years. Romeo Montague was but a fraud by comparison, changing his heart, from Rosaline to Juliet, with the drop of a feathered hat.

In addition, there was always the voyeuristic element. How well he had imagined himself being offered up to science, allowing himself to be transported to some distant operating theater. Claiming to have epileptic tendencies, he would consent, along the dotted line, to certain memory experiments, which would surely have made him a test case. Just as he had read, somewhere, of a man recalling, in toto, an orgasm shared with his lover, so he, by surrendering his will to the mercies of science, would be reunited with his past, playing soccer in the streets of Ipanema, or losing himself to the silken embrace of his beloved Azadina. The surgeon's spatula would seek out all the elements of his persona, uncovering countless hidden mysteries, the better to reveal completely the workings of his psyche. All would be explained, no stone would be left unturned; his past, his future, his complexes, his reflexes, his fate, his destiny would come to the surface at last and his love for Azadina would be proven, empirically, irrefutably, medically! Then he would discover the key to immortality, for the wall of time would have been broken apart, split asunder, by the sledgehammer of science.

The tiny rice-wine cup sat on the table, filled to the brim, a complimentary offering from the staff of the Chung Kock.

Through the window, Aldous saw all manner

of men and animals, some walking along the pavement, up or down, others straying from exotic murals, painted in acrylic, on the walls and ceiling of the restaurant, so that everything around him appeared in a state of flux, making him wonder whether he was inventing it all or it was inventing him. He stared into the cup, at the woman, a recumbent, Oriental beauty, surrounded by tropical vegetation, brought to life by illusion; the waiter poured another shot of liquor into it as soon as Aldous had downed the first, and there she was again, dancing in front of his eyes. And then she disappeared, just as suddenly, where he did not know, he could not say.

He paid up and left. It was late. There was rain on the streets, cool, reflective puddles that made the city somehow smaller, the sky and the cloud and the tops of the buildings crowding him out a little, as if he were back in the restaurant, within the slimy aquarium or lost amid the watery paradise to be found at the bottom of the rice-wine cup. He walked on, glad to have savored the moment, to have held it, like the cup, in his hands. He had been in Paris long enough to have collected an unquantifiable number of such moments; how many of them had he subsequently discarded, left in the gutter, only to see them washed away into the drains and sewers of this great city.

Thought is formalized through language. We think like typewriters. Tap, tap. Tappety. The finger-flattening art of tapping punctuates our movements, as surely as the protective heels of Aldo's Florsheim shoes. People cannot necessarily be read like books, although we often see extracts, the torn pages of thin volumes pasted, at odd intervals and spacings, on their troubled heads.

Aldous, being the exception that proved all rules, was even more, not less, susceptible to this phenomenon. A polyglot of mixed blood, he could converse easily in Portuguese, Italian, English, or French, so that his lofty forehead could be seen, in the moonlight, glowing with the words, "I love Azadina," his hairline receding as if to accommodate the simultaneous translation of his thoughts, the last letter, along with an exclamation mark, disappearing from view, behind his ear.

Entering the rue Saint-Denis at its most southerly point, where it met the rue de Rivoli, he found himself gazing in windows at his reflection, at the shoes, tweed jackets, and trinkets on sale, before looking down at his own shoes, dampened, wet at the uppers, which pulled him forward. His feet felt heavy; he would continue up the street and then pause for a moment, for the time it took to smoke a Lucky Light.

A few people passed, their shoulders hunched in the soft rain; they did not glance at him, but looked forward, or at each other. They were on their way home, for love, and he was striding into the dark, Paris night, determined to pretend that it wasn't raining. Above, the clouds had parted a little; they were moving quickly, heading off to one side or colliding with one another. The rain, quite suddenly, stopped, at the point at which he crossed the rue Réaumur.

It was not inevitable that Azadina should have been there, waiting for him. Yet the figure seated on the fabled bench, the very one on which he had been conceived and on which he had once made love so ardently, could only have been her.

the fabled bench

At the very moment of ejaculation (which is not, in this case "a brief exclamation of surprise," but rather the release of life, thick and white, from Salvatore Radice's quivering prick), the dilapidated bus carrying the tired cast of *Romeo i Julia* from Paris to Warsaw plunged from the secondary road along which it had been shakily traveling and into a mountainous gorge the actors might otherwise have admired, had it not been the dead of night somewhere in Eastern Europe, a place not noted for the quality of its buses, its roads, or even its gorges.

Janusz Wasiutynski and Ludmilla Zawiejski, the bane of every program printer west of the Urals, died instantly, which is to say considerably faster than they had in their penultimate production, as Romeo and Juliet at the Théâtre de l'Odéon, Paris. It was reported the following day that their appearance at that well-known venue, as part of the summer 1959 season had been a "sensation" and a "dramatic surprise," yet hardly as dramatically surprising as their tragic end, on the way home to their loved ones.

Investigators later discovered, apparently, that the wheels of the bus had been unsuitable for the road, their pneumatic grip having been worn down almost to the inner tube, the result of many travels, many journeys, and many curtain calls, the last of which did not so much bring down the house as the bus, so to speak.

We extend our deepest sympathies to the Capulets and the Montagues, most of whom died with the wayward couple, a denouement that not even William Shakespeare, in his darkest, most cynical moments, might have imagined (nor even Luigi da Porta, from whom he stole the plot). Some mitigation of grief might be proferred, however, by those adherents of the Hindu faith, who might read more than coincidence into Aldous Radice's simultaneous conception.

On their second date, prearranged as they parted on the steps of the Théâtre de l'Odéon, the young Italian geologist and the American student met at the Luxembourg Gardens.

First meetings are always nervous affairs, flighty things, Cupid's spent quiver quivering above them, a large question mark poised between two fresh noses. Nobody knows how many couples through history have agreed to meet in the Luxembourg Gardens, or what became of them afterward, tearful partings, invitations to matrimony, promises, promises, all thrown up by the vortex that is love and left aquivering in the autumn air, before being swept up, along with the leaves, by diligent attendants.

They, Aldo's parents, were not unlike many other couples who walked through Paris that day, at the end of August, in 1959; they crossed the river, entering Notre Dame to inspect her rose windows, the blue light of which circled in a beam of dust before falling onto their heads; they lit a candle, then they walked through the Marais, or Jewish quarter, into the place des Vosges (where Salvatore revealed the ambitious side of his nature, pointing to a row of sumptuously appointed apartments and announcing that, one day, he too would be rich) and thence, in a westerly direction, along the rue de Rivoli, not noticing perhaps the bullet holes that surrounded the lower windows of the Hôtel de Ville, the souvenirs of occupation, so much were they noticing each other, the hand of one reaching for its partner after jettisoning a cigarette or the last, flaky particle of an ice cream cone.

Money, at the time, being no object, because

they had none, or very little of it, they bought a sandwich, Gruyère if memory serves, before continuing their excursion. It was evening, quite late in fact, and they elected to stop at a bench on the rue Saint-Denis to take a rest and a breath of air, which was a fraction balmier then, the trees and everything else being freer of dust and smog.

Salvatore had bought a bottle of wine and at this juncture produced it from the voluminous inner pocket of his Lombardian hunting jacket, which his father had given him on his sixteenth birthday and which Aldous would inherit some while later, along with a shotgun and the celebrated photograph (actually in sepia) of Italo Radice, his infamous grandfather.

Those were heady days, when improvisation was a priority: the couple sipped from the green bottle alternately, the young geologist wiping its neck with a handkerchief not dissimilar in shade to the rose window, whose dusty light still somehow shone on them, a benediction, or the first rays of morning and of love.

With nowhere to go, no apparent home for their love (for love it was of the first order, inexplicable, natural), their subsequent gropings should be forgiven, as forgive we must all those who are obliged to do their loving in public places.

There were few people about, this being the dead day of August, Assumption, when everyone flees, together, to be alone. The American girl, Helen, at first reluctant to so much as kiss on the fabled bench, relented, partially through coercion, partially through desire, but mostly because she did not wish to appear too prudish, while the Italian, of course, did all he could to be more Italian than he already was. They both succeeded in their objectives, overcoming their natural and atavistic tendencies to such an extent that copulation became inevitable. Her silken undergarments (Bloomingdale's) were ample, ample enough, certainly, for the maneuver.

"Sex," Salvatore's father had told him, coughing in some distant drawing room, "is a messy business. It can lead to things one may later regret."

That Helen conceived was not, in itself, miraculous. But conceive she did, a fact that no one would later regret, save Aldous, occasionally.

aldous and azadina

Azadina could not quite pinpoint why she followed her own footsteps into the Café Delors. She hadn't been there for ten years; she just happened to be passing along the rue Saint-André-des-Arts, having been to see *The Third Man* at a nearby cinema. Was it to see whether or not she would feel sad, smitten with nostalgia, that vain emotion which is always so generalized, so futile? Touches of sadness, like its counterpart, the pleasure in remembering, materialize from thin or thick air, the willowy wind of a park, the smoke-filled air of a crowded café, so that one smiles, or winces, without really knowing why, or worse, knowing why, yet incorrectly.

Aldous was not in the café, this was only to be expected, but she thought she heard his voice, reaching across time, calling her name. In fact, it was the *patron*, remembering her, still wiping a glass and raising his eyebrows in the familiar manner, as he served her coffee.

The espresso slipped down her throat, serving only to speed up the rate of her sadness, so she ordered a calvados, which she had never drunk before in her life. It burned her insides, making her cough; the *patron* raised his eyebrows. She paid him and left.

She headed back toward her apartment but stopped herself outside l'Hôtel, under the plaques of Borges and Wilde. She didn't want to go back to her little studio, to her books, her trinkets: a brass cat in a box, a photograph of the family, all smiling down at her, a young girl with a doll, sandwiched between lofty, doting parents, the stepped wall of the pyramid behind them, all those objects recalling different people, even though those people were just her, younger, younger still, giving the impression that she might have gone into the wrong apartment by mistake to catch a stranger who, turning her face, was her, only at a different time in her life, when instead of being in love with Aldous, she had pretended to have fallen for a Frenchman, a Dutchman, a fellow Arab.

She looked up. Borges and Wilde must have gone out somewhere; the street felt distinctly void of their presence. So, instead of climbing the six flights to home, she took flight elsewhere.

She saw Aldous before he saw her. She smiled at his ungainly appearance, not because it was funny but because it was unmistakable, the bow tie covered with feathers, the thin, long legs ambling toward her up the wet street. As soon as he spotted her face, underneath her umbrella, he broke into a run, which was odd, because he had never run before. Well, almost never.

"I knew I'd find you here, sooner or later. But I didn't realize it would take ten years and four days." Aldous was out of breath. He stood there, dazed, staring down at Azadina. He pinched himself, and then he pinched her, to check that he wasn't dreaming. Then he pinched a passerby. He would have asked him to take their photograph, but it was dark and he had no camera.

His shadow, cast by the streetlight behind him, had slipped along the pavement from a point midway between his feet, falling a little too brightly perhaps upon Azadina's lap, moving upward so that it nudged her chin and caressed her, at the ear, as she moved forward; she had put the umbrella to one side, brushed her thick, black hair with her hand, and was now standing up. Aldous held her in his arms and kissed her on the lips; her shadow now combined with his so that it fell, neatly, onto the seat of the fabled bench.

"the children of an idle brain"

In another dream, I go to the front door of my apartment. I am back in Paris. By recalling the past in writing this novel, my subconscious is evidently reluctant to take leave of France while I sleep. But I accept everything, of course, because I am a *creative writer.*

Someone has been banging on the front door, for minutes, for hours, for days perhaps. I open it to find a whole crowd of people on the landing, some of whom I recognize, some I do not. There is a maharaja; a crocodile who bears a striking resemblance to Vishnu; Bolu, the lapsed Jain; the girl with the iron over her shoulder; some men dressed in green overalls; and Aldous and Azadina, in skiagraphic form, all waiting in silence. There is also a black cat who, without so much as a by-your-leave, steps nimbly over the threshold and tiptoes into the drawing room. He reminds me of someone, but I can't, for the life of me, put a name to the face.

While the others wait patiently outside, the cat jumps up onto the piano stool, then onto the keyboard, its delicate paws inadvertently creating a tune for my delectation, which I immediately recognize as "Tea for Two," my father's favorite.

I am not necessarily surprised by this intrusion into my privacy, simply puzzled by the scale of it. I am not used to dealing with so many guests. Perhaps there has been some form of communication breakdown? Either that, or a serious road accident has happened somewhere in India. What else could account for such a mixed gathering of spirits?

I go over to the front door and explain, in the most diplomatic terms, that although I greatly appreciate the visitation, I fear I am ill-equipped to entertain en masse. The assembled throng looks at one another earnestly, seeking some guidance and inspiration. I suspect that the maharaja, being the oldest and most senior among them, is their leader and I am soon proved correct, for with the approbative nod of His Highness, the others incline their heads likewise, in unison. Shuffling their feet, they all turn at this point and make their way back along the corridor. I am relieved yet cannot help feeling sorry at the same time, a tinge of guilt, perhaps, exacerbated by my attempts, mostly futile, to make sense of the dream even while it is happening. Part of me rejects this initiative, another part cannot avoid seeking out meaning from these heavily loaded symbols. I am in a quandary and there is nothing I can do about it until I awaken.

I feel especially uncomfortable about the shadow of Aldous and Azadina in my dream, but still I am gratified to see them together. I am not sure whether I am awake or asleep at this point.

My mind wanders. It takes me for a walk, without asking me to leave my bed. In sleep, I enjoy many things, mostly the air, the ventilation of my soul. It is only when I step outside, onto the Paris streets of my imaginings, that I become claustrophobic, almost asphyxiated by the noxious emissions of cars and people. In an earlier dream, I was nearly felled by a motorcyclist, riding on the pavement. His machine was equipped with an apparatus designed for the removal of canine waste, and I was very nearly sucked into the thing! What ignominy! I had to explain to the apparition that, although I was a foreigner, I was still a caste or two above the average piece of dog shit.

I have awakened this morning in good humor, content to have been rescued from my dreams, the attendant imagery of which has brought me closer to that anguish we all feel when we chance upon the void, stumbling from the lip of the volcano or staring up the suction tube of the pavement cleaner. It is only now, upon seeing Paris lit by an

August morning, that I know that I am awake: my conscious memory has taken over from unconscious sleep. What are dreams anyway, but "the children of an idle brain"?

Great wads of literature have been wasted, never to be recycled, on the apparent similarities between fact and fiction. For me, there is none whatsoever. When I retreat from reality, I lock the door from the inside, sealing myself hermetically, to give fantasy full rein. This other world is the stuff of my life; it is the meaning without which there would be no subsequent action. Put another way, fact is what ties me to the present, fiction is what ties me to the future, my destiny.

Some people say that one should never go back. Others say that one should never go forward. Aldous only rediscovered Azadina by going backward. Everyone has his own way of doing things. It's not complicated.

Aldous, of course, did not know that he had been conceived on the fabled bench, nor that, at that very second, Janusz Wasiutynski had been killed in a bus accident, impaled by a spear left in the luggage rack from an earlier production, so that, in one way, Aldous was the reincarnation of an actor, in another, the inadvertent result of lustful opportunism. The odds, as my father would say, are always stacked against the innocent. What are the odds of an egg being fertilized on a Paris bench?

Actors, it is known, are free spirits; they make a living through impersonation. Aldo, or Aldous, had been impersonating himself all his life; he had done it so well it was a wonder he had not been written up in magazines like the one he had read, but not fully understood, in the radiographer's waiting room: "Anybody who enters my life generally ends up in my books!"

Aldous couldn't get that out of his mind. He was particularly intrigued by the idea of "entering" a person's life, as if it were a room, or a building. His own life was a big, open space, with no one in it, except himself and Azadina.

They walked back from the bench, arm in arm, both rather nervously. "But we're heading toward my apartment!" said Aldous. "How do you know where I live?"

"I was just about to say the same thing," said Azadina. And it was true.

They stopped for a moment, halfway between the quai Voltaire and the rue des Beaux-Arts, on the rue des Saints Pères. Then they went to Azadina's; Aldous wanted to see for himself, as if he couldn't quite believe it. Once inside, Azadina took his hand and led him across the tiny studio, to the round window that looked down to the street.

"Can you hear them talking?" she said excitedly. "They're the strangest couple in Paris; apart from us, that is! Wilde is always about 18 and Borges is always old: old and blind. They drink, how do you say, like fishes, and they never go to bed; they wake up the neighbors and are forever banging on the door of the hotel, trying to get the hall porter to open up for them. The lady opposite, Madame Ricardo, has written dozens of letters of complaint, sending them off periodically to the estates of Borges and Wilde, to their French publishers, and to the newspapers. I have read them, she always shows them to me before mailing them; she knows I teach literature so she thinks I am in a good position to advise her on technicalities. I willingly oblige, in fact I really enjoy the task, editing them a little, here and there. She doesn't know this, but I keep copies of them and am hoping, one day, to have them published, in an anthology.

"She has asked my opinion on the notion that Oscar Wilde is a bad influence on Borges, that the 'young flapper,' as she calls him, is corrupting the elderly Argentine. Imagine! I have my own theory, of course: I think that Madame Ricardo, being Argentine herself, is a little biased, in fact I think she's in love and cannot stand the thought of her beloved Borges spending every evening in the company of Wilde. She's even written to City Hall, demanding that they remove Wilde's commemorative plaque, on the grounds that he is a communist and a homosexual. 'Haven't we got enough ghosts about the place, without you ignorant bureaucrats inviting more to stay?' she wrote, in the letter before last. I think she's actually jealous, jealous of a ghost. But the strangest thing of all is that she has picked up the French habit of sending letters of denunciation in all directions. I had one once; in its own way it was beautiful. It accused me of making too much noise when I made love to my husband, when everyone knew that it was not me but the couple below, on the fifth floor, who shake the building with their passion four times a week!"

Aldous and Azadina moved away from the window. They had already slipped away from the view of Paris, the night, from the ghosts of Borges and Wilde (who, in turn, would doubtless slip away at the least expected moment) and were kissing, touching, blending on the silken sheets of the bed fit for a maharaja, so that what had once been two was now a larger, moving picture, a metastasis, the transformation of the overlapping outlines of two lovers into a solid, unbreakable body of darkness, pushed about, this way and that, by the soft bedside light.

And, as it moved, this image, this silhouette, made movements to and from itself, one side encouraging the other to discard its outer layers, its slippery skin, which was, of course, drier to the touch than one might have imagined. Improbable shapes, the subshadows of darkness, thus escaped from it, separating, dividing, disappearing into a corner by the door or up onto the ceiling, two arms gesturing, two sleeves trying to wave down a car on a mountain road, two legs crossing, uncrossing, bending, unbending, the negative of some hapless surfer setting out toward a nonexistent beach (actually Aldo's Brooks Brothers underpants), or a pair of small, delicately pointed breasts, in profile, their nipples massaged by the outstretched fingers of a rabbit's head.

"When I come," said Azadina. "I feel that I am sharing a moment with others. We are all coming together, all of us; we are united for a second in a faraway place."

"And Borges and Wilde? What about them?"

Azadina laughed. "Oh, they're far too busy telling each other stories!"

two months ago

We struggle to find the right words, first with our heart, then with our head, then with our fingers, only to find our thoughts misrepresented on paper. The momentum of veracity is constantly interrupted, the process of creation perverted. According to Mr. Burdoch.

I am now walking around the empty streets of Paris, the Paris of two months ago, hoping to meet Aldous and Azadina, for even I can hardly believe that they are together again.

It occurs to me that everyone, not just me, has been substituting fantasy for reality, the past for the present. This is not a new idea. Writers have been doing it for centuries; it's simply an idea that has achieved universality.

I pause at a café. The sun is bright and strong so that my shadow is reflected in the glass frontage. One of the waiters inside has a video camera, which he is holding apprehensively in both hands, trying to come to grips with its buttons and functions, pointing it at a family of tourists, the patriarch of which, a large, rosy-cheeked Scandinavian, can be seen barking instructions and laughing. The family will always see itself in Paris, remembering the waiter filming them with their camera. It is a moment embued with magic because it is the predestination of their trip to Paris, the *avant vu* and the *déjà vu* of a vacation that only comes to life as it is being recorded by the waiter, so that in seeing it, over and over and over again, whenever they wish, they will be able to see themselves, immortalized, the fulfillment of a fantasy, the symbiosis of past, present, and future, the transference of action into memory and memory into action. The process is ritualistic, profound, banal, ridiculous, and sentimental, simultaneously robbing the family of its collective power to mythologize their vacation, giving evidence, as it does, of its *real* circumstances, so that little Sigmund, 20 years later, upon completing his creative writing course, will be unable to recall his childhood trip to Paris through the filter of his own personality. No approximation of the truth will be permitted. It has happened, it has been filmed, it is irrevocable.

Veni, vidi, video!

I move away from the polemical window and walk on toward the river. I feel like an outcast. I *am* an outcast. I see people walking past me, their faces not revealing a hint of what might be turning in their minds, what moves them, what frightens them, and I feel so alone, so unequivocally alone. I am so used to this feeling now that it rarely makes me sad. Today I received a letter from Aldo, telling me he was in Paris, staying at Hilton's friend's apartment, that he had been in town since the beginning of the month and had tried to reach me. I called the apartment early this morning, but there was no answer. So I have decided to make a little tour of the neighborhood, to see whether he has gone out to a café; it was for this reason that I found myself staring into the café where the waiter was making a home movie.

I remember the last time I saw Aldous; it was in Paris. Of course, we missed meeting the first time. But we did finally meet up, quite by chance, a week or so later. It was August twenty-fifth; I remember because that's my mother's birthday and we drank a toast to her. That was ten years ago. I had spoken to my cousin between not meeting him in the Café de Flore and meeting him afterward; he called me to tell me that he had fallen in love with a girl named Azadina. I was intrigued to meet her, and when I finally did, I was greatly impressed. The two of them spent a week or two, hopelessly in love; they were inseparable. Then Aldo had to go back to the U.S. to college.

I was walking along the rue Saint-André-des-

Arts during that time (I can't remember exactly why; it was a long time ago) in much the same way as I am walking now, just rolling along, staring into windows and daydreaming, stopping to write something in a notebook or chat with an acquaintance who might be passing, when I came across the Café Delors. It amused me to have found it like that, by chance, and I decided to go in to see what it was like. There were one or two tourists there, but in the corner I could see a couple, one obviously American, the other dark-skinned. I recognized Aldo immediately.

What fun we had that afternoon, reminiscing about Ipanema, about going to the theatre to see *Romeo and Juliet*, and about my father losing his money at Saratoga in a photo finish!

Ten Augusts later, I am back in the rue Saint-André-des-Arts, going into a corner store to get a pack of cigarettes. It's a Sunday, but there are still a lot of people about, spilling over from the market on the rue de Seine, tourists mostly, doing what tourists always do, stopping at a corner to turn a map the right way around, orienting themselves so that their cameras point north, or gazing with uncertainty at menu boards outside restaurants where the *patrons* stand in doorways, like pimps.

I walk on, as if in a dream, caught up with this tide of human flotsam, not quite daring to imagine the inevitable, for I know that anniversaries are always providential. An old friend, the Dancer, appears from the shade of a café and we kiss each other on the cheek. He asks me how my writing is going and I tell him that it has gone for the time being. "You are young, you have time. I am old. And I have experience. Things are never quite perfect, but never as bad as they sometimes look. Like a whiskey?" he says, with a smile, pointing to a hip flask in his pocket.

I stare into the faces of the crowd, wondering whether Aldous might have come to the market to buy something, a bottle, a loaf of bread, and then decided to wander over to Notre Dame, whose rose windows so fascinated him the last time he was here. It is at this moment that I pass the Café Delors. It is packed and I stare into it, pressing my nose against the window.

Something, I do not know what, prevents me from going in. I am a natural voyeur; I prefer watching to being watched (I'm sure I would have made a lousy actor). I can see, at the counter, a row of men drinking kier, and taller, younger types elbowing their way through them trying to attract the attention of the *patron*, whose forehead perspires a little with the heat and the exertion of his labors. His wipes his brow with his forearm and then raises his eyebrows, comically, like a character from a silent movie. All the tables are full and I strain my eyes, seeking out my cousin in the gallery of faces, backs of heads, laughing profiles, all caught in the thick, musty air of the café, obscured for one moment, revealed the next, by the passing of new entrants, the floral dress of a summer beauty swishing past them, so that their heads turn again, this way and that, in admiration.

Just beyond the window, not far from the bar, is a couple, in silhouette, their noses almost touching. They are seated near the bar, yet they seem completely oblivious to everything that is going on around them. The man is tall, his elbows are on the table as he leans forward to kiss the girl on the lips. Just a peck, that's all, and then he retreats a little, a smile broadening on his face. I cannot make out the rest of his features, his eyes and nose are cast in the shadow of his Panama hat. The woman opposite him has very short, dark hair, her head is turned away from me a little, so I am frustrated in my attempts to make out her features. Now she moves forward and kisses her partner; then she puts her finger to his nose and laughs.

I have never seen two people so much in love. One sees lovers all the time in Paris; it is a place that always seems full of couples touching each other, stopping in their tracks to kiss, sometimes quite passionately, or simply holding each other, as people do, elsewhere, only when they have bolted the front door from the inside; but in the ten years I have been here, I cannot recall a couple so lost to themselves! This is exaggerated by the business of the café, of course, but also by my own increasingly pronounced sadness at being constantly alone without love, a hand to hold, a shoulder to kiss in the middle of a sticky August night.

When was the last time I sat in a café with a girl and kissed her hand like that! I tell myself that I have learned much in my 34 years, I have read plenty of books, I have lived every second of those years, feeling the cold seep into my bloodstream or catching my breath at a sunset as it soaked the sky with blood, a gaping wound that terrified me even as it startled me with its beauty. Yet I don't think I have learned anything about love. Anything at all. I would gladly trade everything I have or have not for the *need* of it, for it is that which I have lacked for so long; I would give up all my past and all my future, all the days and nights of Brahma, each day and each night lasting 1,000 years of the gods and each year of the gods corresponding to 120 centuries of man, for just one second or a fraction of a second, spent lost within the collective shadow of those two, as they lean across the table once again to kiss.

I step into the café, drawn by the aura of the couple. I make my way to the bar and order a Pernod. I take a sip; it fortifies me. I turn back toward the crowded tables, hoping to catch a glimpse of the man with the Panama and the girl with the short hair. But they have gone. I am angry at myself for having let them out of my sight. I drain the glass of Pernod and shake my head. There is a tap on my shoulder. The man with the Panama is looking into my eyes. It is Aldous, of course.

"Lenny! At last!"

We embrace. The woman is laughing behind us. She has bent down to pick up the hat, which fell to the floor as I clutched my cousin. It is Azadina.

"Leonard! We were talking about you. Just now. We were wondering what happened to you. What did happen to you?"

"Azadina!"

"Come and sit down, Lenny. You look shocked. Let's have a drink, shall we?"

They lead me to the table. Aldous finds a chair for me and then disappears to get the drinks.

"Azadina! You've had all your hair cut off. You look different. But still beautiful."

"My hair? That was a long time ago. Years ago."

Aldous returns with a bottle and three glasses. "You got my letter? What's wrong with your damned telephone?"

"Couldn't make the bill. You know how it is. Or maybe you wouldn't, Aldo," I add with a smile.

"Need some money? I'll pay it. At least then I'll be able to call you up now and then."

"I can't believe it!" I exclaim, shaking my head.

"What can't you believe?"

"I knew we'd meet, sooner or later. But what's just crossed my mind is that today is a Sunday."

"What about it?"

"Well, what date does that make it?"

"It's the twenty-fifth, Lenny," said Aldous, pulling out his diary.

"Did the old man give you that, Aldo? It's like the ones he gets from Kagan's."

"Yeah. He gave it to me. Always does. Every year."

"Give it to me! Let's have a look. Jesus, it *is* the twenty-fifth. We met on this day, at about this time, exactly ten years ago. We'd better raise our glasses. It's mom's birthday!"

We spend the afternoon in the café, doing what people always do when they meet after a long absence; talking about the last time they met, or the time before that.

"And what about the creative writing, Lenny? How's that going?" asks Aldo. "I've still got your poems."

"I'm trying to figure out what uncreative writing is at the moment. I still haven't got a publisher. And I still teach English as a foreign language, which is becoming more and more foreign the more I teach it."

We finish the bottle of Chablis. Aldo gets up to order another. And I stare at Azadina dumbstruck, waiting for her to ask me something.

Man has a wicked eye, it follows the contours

of a woman's body quite shamelessly, darting from
one promontory to the next with impunity, taking
in the firmness of the breasts, the nipples of
which somehow point to him through the scarlet
silk of her shirt or blouse (Oh, Azadina!), continuing to the folds of her thighs and, should he be
lucky enough, assessing the quality of the hips and
legs with all the rapidity of a laser beam, of the
sort one can also use to survey the works of great
masters, so that, in *stilleven met boeken*, for example, we note a great deal of traffic about the head
of the subject. This laser eye suffers no censor-
ship, it continues its work unheeded, moving up
and down, from side to side, motivated not by the
exigencies of geometry nor by any particular aes-
thetic, but for the most part by an abstracted
form of lust, along with the desire to categorize
objectively so that comparisons can be made with
others: the shape of the chin referred to another,
or still another, seen earlier, in another place, or
the size of the mouth and thickness of the lips,
which the observer might imagine, if he so wishes,
in contact with his own features, not all of them
visible during the daytime. And all this, in the
time it takes to respond to Azadina's question, as
Aldous returns to the table with a fresh bottle of
wine.

"No, Azadina. I never got married. I was looking too hard."

oh, azadina!

It was Aldo who suggested the trip to Provence. He wanted to go to Saint-Rémy, to visit the asylum where van Gogh once found himself incarcerated. He told me he had always wanted to go there and that he had been discussing it with Azadina. She still had some time off before having to go back to teach at school.

I was flattered that they invited me, genuinely pleased, despite the fact that I have a particular aversion to traveling with a couple. One so often finds oneself in the invidious position of referee, or even worse, having to collaborate with one side or the other. Ones status is never clear, the man might be jealous, the woman might be attractive, they might be fighting, they might be too happy together, making one feel like an interloper. But what was I thinking? This was my cousin, dear Aldo! And Azadina, the lovely Azadina!

There was, of course, the embarrassment

over money, of which I had so little, hardly enough to pay for my train ticket. But then, this was not such a problem. Aldous and I had an understanding. We felt, being Italian, being *family*, that blood was thicker than water. He was like a brother to me. My father had handled (albeit with a certain profligacy) the fortune that Aldo had inherited from his parents, held in trust until his twenty-first birthday. I had never accepted money from him unless I really needed it, and I had hardly seen him since my college years, during which my father took care of my financial problems. Aldo had bought me a typewriter once, that I remember well. I was 18, I think. Yes, I felt embarrassed, for he was only 15 at the time. But I was touched by his kindness, for kindness it was. It is easy to be generous with money when you have a lot of it. What is more difficult is spending some time reflecting on another's needs and satisfying them, suspending one's own ego for a moment or two.

Aldous asked me to reserve three seats on the train and to think about a hotel where we could stay. We would go for three or four days, have a look around, get out of the city and take in some fresh air. It had the air of an adventure, of a memory to be made, and its timing, as far as I was concerned, could not have been more opportune. After all, I had had a pretty difficult year, with little respite. It is true I had managed to take a short break earlier in the month, invited to someone's cottage in Brittany. But that had been a disaster. She was an ex-lover, and we argued on the first day; she told me that I was indulgent and I told her that *everyone* was indulgent. We didn't speak for the rest of the weekend and came back to Paris on separate trains.

Yes. It was time for something a little different. I accepted their invitation.

harm

What an *age* ago it seems! An Australian dawn is breaking, and the night through which I have just traveled separates me, not simply from yesterday, or the day before that, but from all my yesterdays. I go across to the window of the apartment, here in Tamarama, and I gaze, with a certain relief, at the large-paned glass of sea and sky, all neatly framed, so that breaking waves and cloud appear cut, dissected, pasted, and glued upon it, blocking out everything else. I look down from the balcony, into the earth and through, to the other side, so that I can now see myself, an antipodean view of the uncreative writer, walking away from the Café Delors a little drunkenly, shaking Aldo's hand and kissing Azadina on the cheek (what sweet perfume!), arranging to meet them at Azadina's apartment, on the way to the Gare de Lyon and Provence.

My legs carry me forth in the same way that they did then, yet as if for the very first time. Yesterday I was a quadruped, like the cat, Bastet, tripping the keys of an old pianoforte, sipping milk from a saucer or hiding in shadow, asleep. Today, I am a biped. Who knows, tomorrow I could be a monoped, hopping about on the landing while I wait to use the bathroom.

I am like an evolutionary drawing, halfway between a monster and a robot; my inner history is personal, private, particular, yet my outer skin, my appearance, makes me part of an entire species. I am a part of the human race but, of course, like Groucho, I have a natural aversion to belonging to any club that would accept me as a member. But even with Aldo dead and buried, I still have one or two friends. The Dancer.

And Harm, the art thief.

I ran into Harm on the way home from the Café Delors. He was in the process of being extradited to Holland for his part in the theft, three months earlier, of *stilleven met boeken* from the van Gogh Museum, Amsterdam. I have already told you that the cover for this book was his idea. Perhaps it would shock you to learn that the *book itself*, in a way, was also his idea.

We went to a café on the rue de Buci that afternoon. I had an espresso to sober me up after all the Chablis I had drunk with Aldous and Azadina. We chatted, earnestly, about Harm's predicament. I had only known him a couple of years, he was just someone one met occasionally, in the street; but I liked him a good deal nevertheless, this lofty Dutchman with a faraway look in his eye.

I knew he was mad about van Gogh but I didn't know until then that he was an art thief. Maybe he was more of a prankster; he was certainly mysterious. That was the last time I saw him before leaving France. He's probably in some jail in Holland by now.

It was strange running into him just after leaving Aldous and Azadina and planning the trip to Saint-Rémy. But what can I say? The world is small; and Paris is even smaller, especially from where I am now.

Harm told me that he would probably get off quite lightly, as he hadn't been the ringleader. He was fairly sure that he would be treated leniently. He had a good attorney who was convinced that he would be judged as "not being of sound mind." Looking into those deep blue eyes, I could see that the attorney was on the right track. Harm produced the postcard of *stilleven met boeken* (I think we'd stepped out onto the street by this point) and, waving it in my direction, told me that it was the perfect cover for a novel: a love story. I agreed. He spoke about van Gogh for a while, a glazed look in his eyes, as if he had gone into a trance. "The reason van Gogh was the greatest painter who ever lived is quite simple: he was the most *passionate*."

"Yes, Harm," I replied, as he grasped my wrist with his hand and slapped the postcard against my chest.

"Take the card, Lenny. It's yours. Just know that *stilleven met boeken* is the finest and most subtle of all his paintings. It is magical, for over a hundred years it has been waiting for someone to complete it, to add the words to the story. And, if you look into it carefully enough, you will see the shadow of someone falling onto it, through the frame. That person is the hero of the story. Find him, Lenny! Find him! He's out there, somewhere."

the north star

The North Star can be seen quite clearly, if
you happen to be looking in the right direction. It is nearly seven centuries away from us,
yet it is clearer, brighter, sharper than the bedroom light, shrouded in tasseled shades, that
falls tactlessly onto the bare shoulders of Madame Ricardo. She removes her dress, a limp
and wrinkled body appears, just long enough
for the light to travel across the street to Azadina's apartment, and then she covers herself
within the silken folds of a chinoiserie gown,
on which embroidered figures seem to float, to
dance in the dim, sinister interior of the room:
faraway creatures summoned by the sleep of a
nearby infant, capricious, flighty, elusive, only
there but for the grace of a trained, inner eye.

As usual, she is preparing herself for an
important visitor, lighting her sticks of in-
cense, transporting the little brass tray, replete
with cocktail glasses, port, and modest eata-
bles, from the kitchen to the salon, and

putting the finishing touches to her face, two thin lines of pencil to tautened eyebrows, a dash of powder to her tired cheeks. The stage is set for her seduction of the great, blind writer, Señor Borges.

If it were at all possible to travel in space, as well as in time, and should Madame Ricardo have permitted such an intrusion, we would be able to see from the gloomy window of her apartment the two faces of Aldous and Azadina peering from a small, rose circle, the window of the studio opposite. But that would be to confuse those watching with those being watched, to upset the balance between subject and object. The empty street between them, a gulf, an abyss containing nothing but dust and darkness, becomes as great and as impenetrable a void as the one that separates us from the stars; yet we are so close to each other, we who watch, this way or that, from the imaginary spot that is our vantage point, somewhere between the two.

The hall porter, hearing a noise, steps out onto the street, shakes his head, and goes back into the hotel. And above, their arms intertwined, Aldous and Azadina now settle their gaze southward above the rose window, so that they do not see the old man entering Madame Ricardo's apartment; neither do they see the prescient spirit of the North Star, for it is now behind them, beyond the boundaries of this City of Light. The curtains are drawn so that no one, except the participants, will know what is happening or what is about to happen. Love shuts the door and we slip away, for a moment, into the night.

A psychic once boasted to Aldous that she could even rearrange his dreams if she wanted to. She got what she deserved. Aldous dreamed her up and then threw her off a cliff. "Rearrange that!" he called out to her, in his sleep. Azadina awoke, with a start.

"Are you all right, Aldo?"

"Just a dream, Azadina. Just a dream."

Azadina rubbed her eyes. "I have a confession to make, Aldo, about Madame Ricardo. It's not really true that she writes letters of complaint to City Hall, complaining about the ghost of Oscar Wilde. It's me. I made it all up. I have been watching her for five years, preparing herself for the visitor who never comes to her in the night. I write the letters. It's my way of making sense of what I see. By making her fall in love with Borges, I have given her the lover she dreams about, every time she puts on her gown and brings in the tray of port."

She kissed Aldous on the forehead and went back to sleep in his arms. Aldous stayed awake for the rest of the night, hardly moving, thinking of how his life had changed from solitude to companionship, from thinking of Azadina to being with Azadina to being *in* Azadina. And, because he was now seen by her, witnessed by her, he had become, in a way, her invention, the physical metamorphosis of her idea of him. His time was no longer private, kept to himself. He was with her constantly; since their reunion on the fabled bench, they had not been apart for a minute. His own world, the one he had carried about on his shoulders, had slipped away, out of orbit, the orbit defined by the new star that was Aldous and Azadina. The only reference he had of himself now was the reflection caught in the mirror on the wall opposite the bed, or divided by the shop windows he passed in the street below, when the two of them set out in the morning to rediscover Paris together. Apart from that, the only view he had of himself, so inferior to the one enjoyed by Azadina, was the tiny fraction of his face, the lips, when pursed, the blurred side of an angular nose and the body, foreshortened, seen from the chest down, rubbing itself with a towel or trying to undo the knots left tied on his Florsheim shoes.

epilogue

Azadina and I have acquired a black kitten,
whom we have christened Bastet, after the
Egyptian goddess sometimes known for her
benevolence, at other times, her misanthropy,
when put in the same basket as the lioness,
Sakhmet. Most deities have their good and
their bad sides, like people. The interesting
thing about Bastet, our cat, is that she bears,
despite her gender, a remarkable similarity to
Aldous. She is tall, aloof, and happy to be left
alone. Cats are independent spirits. I know I
am mixing my mythology here, but I like to
think that there is, perhaps, a little of my
cousin in this affable quadruped.

Azadina and I were not sorry to quit
France after Aldo's tragic death in the garden
of the Hotel van Gogh, Saint-Rémy-de-
Provence. We both felt like a fresh start. She
did not accompany me to New York for the
funeral; we didn't think that would have been
appropriate. In fact, it is just as well she stayed

in Paris, to give up the leases on our respective apartments and put our personal effects into storage. She was waiting for me when I arrived here, as I had decided to spend two weeks with my parents in Brooklyn. Yes, we were apart for a while, but we survived it.

I cannot honestly tell you why we chose Australia. As I have intimated, it is the last place on earth I thought I would ever end up. It just happened that I ran into an old friend from college in Manhattan one night, who had just returned from down under and was enthusiastic. An agrarian economist, he had spent a year lecturing in Sydney and knew quite a few people. By chance, one of his friends knew of an apartment by the ocean at Tamarama.

I know Azadina misses Paris occasionally. I'm sure we'll go back one day. But I cannot say when. Australia has been very kind to us. I must say it's been a real tonic for me, getting the chance to sit down to write the novel I always dreamed of writing. I am also delighted that my editor likes the cover.